LOOK, LISTEN AND LOVE

Their brilliant plan, Tempera Rothley reflected, had brought utter disaster.

Left penniless by the death of Lord Rothley, she and her beautiful young stepmother had no hope but to marry as soon as possible. Lady Rothley's chance came first: a house party in the south of France hosted by the elegant, eligible Duke of Chevingham.

The invitation created one problem: the Duke expected his guest to bring her Lady's maid. Hiring one was out of the question. Tempera would have to accompany her stepmother disguised as a maid.

Here she was—miserable amidst the lush beauty of the Riviera—a frightened, insignificant Lady's maid falling in love with a Duke.

BARBARA CARTLAND

Bantam Books by Barbara Cartland
Ask your bookseller for the books you have missed

Barbara Cartland
Look, Listen and Love

BANTAM BOOKS
TORONTO · NEW YORK · LONDON

LOOK, LISTEN AND LOVE
A Bantam Book | May 1977

ISBN 0–553–10972–3

Published simultaneously in the United States and Canada

Bantam Books are published by Bantam Books, Inc. Its trade-
mark, consisting of the words "Bantam Books" and the por-
trayal of a bantam, is registered in the United States Patent
Office and in other countries. Marca Registrada. Bantam
Books, Inc., 666 Fifth Avenue, New York, New York 10019.

PRINTED IN THE UNITED STATES OF AMERICA

Author's Note

Virgin of the Rocks, in the Louvre in Paris, was painted about 1485 and is the earliest of the pictures which Leonardo da Vinci is known to have completed.

It was the centre panel of an altar piece commissioned by the Confraternity of the Immaculate Conception in Milan.

Madonna in the Church, by Jan van Eyck, 1380–1441, is in the Dahlem Museum, Berlin. *St. George and the Dragon,* by Raphael, is in the National Gallery of Art, Washington.

Portrait of a Young Girl, by Petrus Cristus, 1400–1473, is in the Stault Museum, Berlin. He was a contemporary and perhaps a pupil of Jan van Eyck but in comparison he seems to have been almost deaf to the voices of the spirit. Only in this really noble and suggestive work can we see the spiritual sensitivity which is so moving in all Jan van Eyck's pictures.

Chapter One

1904

"Tem . . . pera! Tem . . . pera!"

The excited voice rang out in the small house and Tempera hastily put down the gown she was sewing to run to the top of the stairs.

In the hall below she could see her Stepmother looking like an exotic bird of Paradise in a feather-trimmed hat and green gown beneath a short fur coat.

Her face was upturned to the top of the staircase as she cried breathlessly:

"Oh, Tempera, I have done it! I have done it! Come down—I must tell you about it."

Without replying, Tempera ran down the stairs and followed her Stepmother into the small front room.

Lady Rothley pulled off her coat and flung it on a chair, then clasping her hands together she said:

"He has asked me! He has actually asked me to go to the South of France and stay in his Château!"

Tempera gave a little cry of delight.

"Oh, *Belle-mère,* how thrilling! The Duke has finally succumbed to your charms! I thought he would!"

"I was doubtful," Lady Rothley said frankly.

She took off her velvet hat as she spoke and

1

stared at herself in the mirror over the mantelpiece, seeing her red-gold hair above a very beautiful face.

"Tell me what the Duke said," Tempera asked from behind her. "And when do you go?"

"On Friday," Lady Rothley replied.

"Friday?"

The exclamation was startled.

"But *Belle-mère,* that gives us only three days to get everything ready."

"I do not care if it is three minutes," Lady Rothley replied. "He has asked me, I am to stay in his Château near Nice, and nothing else is of any consequence."

"No . . . of course not," Tempera agreed doubtfully, "but you will want clothes."

Lady Rothley turned from the contemplation of her reflection in the mirror to say:

"Of course I shall want clothes, and I shall also need the money with which to buy them."

She saw the expression on her Stepdaughter's face and went on:

"You know the things I wore last summer are in rags, and it will be quite warm in the South of France at this time of the year. After all, it is March and it can even be quite hot."

"I know, *Belle-mère,*" Tempera agreed. "But as you well know, it is going to be difficult to find very much money!"

"Yes, I know," Lady Rothley agreed. "Is there nothing left to sell?"

"Only the one drawing which we were keeping against a 'rainy day.'"

"Then sell it! Sell it!" Lady Rothley cried. "This is a 'rainy day,' and I am sure—yes, I am absolutely sure—that the Duke is enamoured of me."

Her Stepdaughter did not speak and after a moment she went on:

"He said today that I was pure Titian. Who was Titian?"

Tempera laughed and the look went from her face.

"*Belle-mère,* you must know who Titian was! And

the Duke is right. You are exactly like his picture of *Venus with the lute-player,* and perhaps too the *Venus of the Mirror.*"

"Is that a compliment?" Lady Rothley asked doubtfully.

"A great compliment!" Tempera replied, and liked the smile which lit up her Stepmother's face.

It was true, she thought, and the Duke was right. Her Stepmother did look exactly like Titian's models in the two pictures she had mentioned.

Lady Rothley had the same fair-gold hair, the same round face, warm lips, and large enquiring eyes, and the same voluptuous figure.

The exception was that Lady Rothley pulled in her waist until it was tiny to accentuate the full curves of her bosom and her hips.

The S-bend was due to the influence of an American, Charles Dana Gibson. It was attained by a corset boned so as to make the torso appear hardly to belong to a woman's lower anatomy.

Lady Rothley managed this to perfection and as she was in fact a very beautiful woman, Tempera was not surprised that the Duke of Chevingham found her attractive.

When he first invited her Stepmother to his parties they had not attached any particular significance to it, since the parties at Chevingham House were famous for all the beautiful women who congregated there.

But after one or two invitations to Balls and Receptions, Lady Rothley had been included in intimate dinner-parties which were the envy of every Society socialite.

That was where both Tempera and her Stepmother thought, with satisfaction, she was most likely to meet a suitable second husband.

Even so, they had not aspired as high as the Duke. But now with this invitation to the South of France it appeared that he might be personally interested.

"I must have clothes—beautiful clothes!" Lady Rothley said firmly.

Tempera replied without hesitation:

"Of course, *Belle-mère,* I will go now and take the Dürer drawing to Papa's friend at the National Gallery. He has always admired it, and if he does not buy it himself he will put me in touch with someone who will."

"While you are doing that," Lady Rothley reflected, "perhaps I would be wise to go at once to Lucille and see what she can have ready in the time."

There was only a slight hesitation before Tempera agreed.

She knew that Madame Lucille's flowing tea-gowns and beautifully moulded evening-gowns became her Stepmother better than anything another dress-maker could provide.

At the same time, Lucille was very expensive.

They were, however, both aware of a sense of urgency, and without saying any more Tempera ran upstairs to her room to put on her hat and coat.

Then she entered her father's Study and took down from the wall the sole remaining picture.

There were marks on the wallpaper which showed only too clearly that everything else had been sold.

She might have anticipated, Tempera often thought, that when her father died they would be left with no money.

She at least had the common sense to realise how little he actually possessed, while her Stepmother had always lived in a world of fantasy where nothing as mundane as money ever encroached.

Because Sir Francis Rothley always associated with the most important people, was always in demand in the great houses that held world-famous treasures, their own lack of money did not seem to matter.

Not until he died, when the small income he made as a Trustee and Advisor to various Galleries died with him.

It was Tempera who made a list of their assets and forced her Stepmother to face the fact that it was going to be very difficult to live on what they possessed.

"How can we manage?" Lady Rothley had asked helplessly.

She had never, her Stepdaughter thought, faced reality in the whole of her sheltered life.

Alaine had been brought up in the country, the daughter of a well-bred but undistinguished Country Squire. She had become engaged when she was twenty to a man who after nearly a year's engagement had been killed in India.

Made miserable by this tragedy, there was no-one else in her life until when she was over twenty-four she came to London to stay with an aunt and quite by chance encountered Sir Francis Rothley at a dinner-party.

He was bowled over by her beauty, and having been widowed for only a year threw all precautions to the wind and asked Alaine to marry him.

She accepted him with alacrity, not only because he was a way of escape from the dull existence she had been leading, but also because, Tempera thought, she loved him in her own way.

Alaine was quite incapable of very deep feelings, nor, despite her looks, was she a passionate woman.

She was good-tempered, charming, and in many ways extremely stupid.

She wanted everyone to love her and so she was never prepared to voice a positive opinion or contradict anyone else's.

She just wanted to sail serenely through life, and the fact that men should think her beautiful was all she asked of the present and the future.

It would have been impossible for anyone, least of all Tempera, not to like her Stepmother, and although she was so much younger she realised that Alaine was like a child she must look after, a débutante who could not fend for herself.

But it was Alaine who actually thought of a solution to their problems.

She had stared blindly at the figures as Tempera tried to explain what they would have between them after her father's funeral was paid for and his debts met.

"We shall have to get married!"

Her Stepdaughter stared at her in surprise.

"Married?" she ejaculated.

It seemed somehow wrong to speak of such a thing when her father had just died.

"There is no other solution," Lady Rothley said, spreading out her hands. "We both need husbands to provide for us. Besides, why should either of us wish to live alone?"

It was, Tempera thought afterwards, the only sensible thing her Stepmother had ever suggested, but it was she, of course, who saw the difficulties.

"If it is a question of clothes," she said tentatively, "there will not be enough money to dress us both."

The two women's eyes met across the table and it was Tempera who spoke first.

"You must get married first, *Belle-mère,* then perhaps you will be able to help me a little."

"Of course I will help you, dearest," Alaine Rothley replied, "and you are right. As I am the elder, I must find myself another husband—and quickly!"

She gave a complacent little smile as she added:

"It should not be difficult."

"No, of course not," Tempera answered.

At the same time, she was wise enough to know that a beautiful widow without money would attract all sorts of men, but only a very few of them, like her father, would be prepared to offer marriage.

She had not taken any part in Social life; in fact it would have been unheard of for any young girl who had not made her début to do so.

But she had met some of the important and distinguished men who asked her father's advice on Art and who sometimes visited him at home instead of his going to their houses.

During her mother's illness and after her death her father had talked to her about them, explaining who they were, usually of course concentrating on their valuable pictures.

But sometimes, in his inimitable, witty way he gave her a thumb-nail sketch of their lives and their interests.

Tempera was very intelligent and had a retentive mind.

She remembered what her father had told her about these personages of distinction, just as she remembered his stories of the personal lives of the great Master-Painters of the past.

Her Stepmother's interests lay entirely in the Social world of the present.

She knew of each new beauty who was pursued by the King, which man had laid his heart at the feet of the beautiful Duchess of Rutland, and who was currently in love with the pink, white, and gold loveliness of Lady Curzon.

It was a fascinating world of glamour and luxury, but to Tempera it was as unreal as the glass bubbles one could buy which contained a snow scene.

Yet because there was a streak of practical common sense in her, it was she who directed and produced, as if on a stage, her beautiful Stepmother.

It was Tempera who saw that Alaine Rothley was in the right place at the right moment, so that she could be the recipient of the invitations that were so important to her.

At Ranclagh, Ascot, the opening of the Royal Academy, Henley, and even at the fourth of June at Eton, Lady Rothley was to be seen looking amazingly alluring, her full mouth smiling and her blue eyes shining in a manner which most men found irresistible.

And far more strict than any ambitious Mama, Tempera sorted out the men who pursued such a Vision persistently but with very different intentions from that which she and Lady Rothley required.

"I met the most charming man last night," Lady Rothley had said two days ago when Tempera brought

her breakfast in bed. "He never left my side. When
he kissed my hand good-night my heart fluttered—it
did really, Tempera!"

"What was his name?" Tempera enquired.

"Lord Lemsford. Have you heard of him?"

"I am not sure," Tempera answered. "I will look
him up in Debrett."

She put the breakfast-tray down beside her Stepmother and Lady Rothley sat up eagerly to pour out the
coffee and lift the covered dish to see what lay beneath it.

"Oh, Tempera, only one egg?" she exclaimed reproachfully.

"You know, *Belle-mère,* that I have had to let out
your gowns by at least an inch," Tempera replied.

"But I am hungry," Lady Rothley said plaintively.
"I am always hungry."

"You eat far too much of those rich meals when
you are out," Tempera said firmly. "You must diet a
little when you are at home . . . besides, it is more
economical."

Lady Rothley did not answer.

She was gobbling up her egg and thinking that
she would spread the two pieces of toast that Tempera
allowed her thickly with butter and add several spoon-
fuls of marmalade.

She liked eating; at the same time, she wanted to
keep her small waist, as she knew it was one of her
most distinctive attractions.

But it was difficult—very difficult—when everything tasted so delicious and the food at the parties
where she was entertained was so superlative.

No Edwardian hostess could lag behind another
when it came to hospitality.

A few minutes elapsed before Tempera came back
from her father's Study, where the books of reference
were kept.

Most of them referred to Art, but he had a copy
of Debrett because it had been important that when

Tempera addressed letters to the distinguished noblemen who sought his advice she did it correctly.

As she entered her Stepmother's bed-room, Lady Rothley looked up expectantly.

"Well?" she asked.

"He is thirty-nine," Tempera replied, "has a house in London and one in Somerset, belongs to all the best Clubs, and . . ." she paused for effect, ". . . a wife and five children!"

Lady Rothley gave a scream of annoyance.

"Every married man should have a brand on his forehead, or a chain round his wrist," she said peevishly.

Tempera laughed.

"Never mind, *Belle-mère,* perhaps he will get his wife to invite you to a smart party where you will meet some eligible bachelors."

"But he was so charming," Lady Rothley pouted. "I might have guessed, might I not, that there would be something wrong?"

"Like the man you met last week whom we learnt was practically bankrupt," Tempera replied. "I had my suspicions about him when I saw that he belonged only to one not-very-important Club."

* * *

As Tempera set out towards the National Gallery, taking a horse-drawn omnibus to Trafalgar Square, she tried not to mind that the last memento of her father must be sacrificed on the altar of fashion.

She had kept back the Dürer drawing because she loved it and also because, as she had said when they sold his other picture:

"We must have something in reserve for a 'rainy day.'"

She had been thinking as she spoke that either her Stepmother or herself might become ill, that the roof might need repair, or, which would be a worse disaster, that Agnes would wish to retire.

They would never be able to acquire another servant so cheaply, Tempera was well aware of that.

Besides, because Agnes had been with her mother until she died, Tempera was extremely fond of the old woman and could not imagine the small house in Curzon Street without her.

But Agnes was seventy-seven and the day was undoubtedly dawning when she would no longer be able to carry on keeping the majority of the rooms clean and cooking their frugal meals.

Tempera cooked when anything special was required but she had so much to do for her Stepmother that she had little time for anything else.

Although a basic number of Lady Rothley's gowns since she came out of mourning were bought from dressmakers, it was Tempera who trimmed her delightfully glamorous hats far more cheaply than a Milliner could.

It was Tempera who pressed, darned, and cleaned, and Tempera who by the judicious use of new ribbons and added flowers or frills could make an old gown look like new.

When she returned home it was after six o'clock and she knew that the shops would be shut. She was therefore not surprised to find her Stepmother lying on the sofa in the Drawing-Room on the first floor.

She looked like a recumbent Venus and her eyes were closed. But when Tempera opened the door she raised her head and asked quickly:

"How much did you get?"

"Seventy-five pounds!" Tempera replied.

Lady Rothley gave a little cry of delight and sat up.

"Seventy-five pounds! That is wonderful!"

"We must not spend it all . . . we really must not, *Belle-mère*," Tempera ventured.

She saw the expression on her Stepmother's face and said:

"I was thinking on the way back that if we put twenty-five pounds aside for any emergency, you could have the rest."

"Well, I suppose fifty pounds is better than nothing!" Lady Rothley said grudgingly.

"I can trim the hats you had last summer so that no-one would ever recognise them," Tempera said, "and I was thinking that if we put some new white lace on that gown you wore at Ascot it would look quite different, and the colour suits you so well."

As she spoke she realised that her Stepmother was not listening.

It was so unlike her when clothes were being discussed that she said quickly:

"What is it? There is something you have not told me."

Lady Rothley looked uncomfortable, then said:

"The Duke expects me to bring a lady's-maid."

Tempera was still for a moment. Then she sat down in a chair.

"Did he actually say so?"

"Of course! He said: 'If you and your maid will be at Victoria Station at ten o'clock on Friday morning, Colonel Anstruther will be there to look after you.'"

"Is that his Comptroller?" Tempera asked.

"Yes—a charming man. I have met him several times at Chevingham House. He is a gentlemen, of course, and the Duke seems to rely on him in every way."

They were evading the main issue and they both knew it. After a pregnant silence Tempera said:

"Is it absolutely . . . essential for you to take a lady's-maid?"

"How can I go without one?" Lady Rothley asked. "You know I cannot manage by myself, and all the other women guests will have one as a matter of course."

"It is not going to be easy," Tempera replied. "Apart from the expense, I shall have to instruct her, and there is very little time."

"I am sure you will be able to find someone good from the Domestic Agency in Mount Street," Lady Rothley said confidently.

"You could say that your maid was ill, or too old, like poor Agnes," Tempera suggested. "Then perhaps Colonel Anstruther would find you a French maid, or one of the housemaids could look after you."

"Not a French maid!" Lady Rothley gave a little scream. "You know how bad my French is. I would never be able to make her understand, and besides, I should feel so embarrassed arriving with a pile of luggage and no-one to look after it."

"Very well," Tempera said, "but it means one gown less, you realise that?"

Lady Rothley pouted.

"I cannot do with less than I have ordered already. I am sure Dottie Barnard will be in the party, and I have told you how smart she is with a new gown to wear every night, and jewels which eclipse the chandeliers."

"But Sir William is one of the richest men in England," Tempera replied in a cold voice.

"Which is why he is so friendly with the King and all those Rothschilds," Lady Rothley said. "Oh, Tempera, if only we had some money!"

"If you marry the Duke you will have all you require and a great deal more besides," Tempera answered.

"Then I refuse—absolutely refuse—to go to the South of France looking like a beggar-maid, although Heaven knows, Tempera, I do not want some stuffy, supercilious maid complaining she has to darn my clothes because they are falling into rags."

Lady Rothley threw herself back against the cushions on the sofa with a little sound of exasperation.

"The trouble is, Tempera, I want so many new things, and it is only because of you that I have managed to hold together those I have."

"I know, but we must try to find an understanding maid who is skilful with her needle."

"She is certain to grumble and complain," Lady Rothley groaned. "Like that poisonous woman just before your father died. 'Really, M'Lady, your underclothes look like a jig-saw puzzle!' she used to say. How I disliked her!"

Tempera laughed.

"She did not stay long, and it was only when she had gone that we found all your things that she refused to mend bundled into the back of a drawer."

"For goodness' sake, do not get me anyone like her!" Lady Rothley pleaded. "And there was that other horror—what was her name?"

"I think you must mean Arnold," Tempera replied.

"That is right—Arnold! She was always having her tea whenever I wanted her and refused to appear until the 'sacred cup' was finished."

Tempera laughed again.

"I see I shall have to find a maid with no partiality for tea."

"They all have that," Lady Rothley said. "It is the 'drug of the Servants' Hall,' but when I said so to your father he replied it was preferable to gin! I did not think it was much of an answer."

"I expect Papa was thinking of how much gin was consumed by servants in the eighteenth century," Tempera replied, "and of course in all the big houses they still drink an enormous amount of beer."

"The servants can drink champagne for all I care, as long as they are there to wait on me, but I am dreading the thought of this lady's-maid."

Tempera did not answer.

She was taking off the plain hat which she had worn to go to the National Gallery and smoothing down the waves of her dark auburn hair.

She was very slim and graceful, but she looked very different from the fashionable women with whom her Stepmother associated.

As if to accentuate the difference, instead of her hair being swept up in waves across the front, she drew it back from her forehead into a bun at the back of her head.

Only when she was busy did small tendrils curl

round her face to soften the severity of the style, which was reminiscent of the Madonnas painted by the early Italian Masters.

Tempera, hardly seeing her reflection in the mirror, pushed aside a few curls; she was thinking of her Stepmother and the problem of finding a lady's-maid who would suit her.

Only Tempera realised in what bad repair were so many of her Stepmother's underclothes, and she had to darn and darn her stockings, rather than throw them away as any other Lady of Fashion would have done.

The same thoughts must have been running through Lady Rothley's head because suddenly with a little groan she said from the sofa:

"Oh, Tempera, if only you could come with me."

"I wish I could," Tempera answered. "I would give anything to see the South of France. Papa often described it to me and once he actually stayed at Lord Salisbury's Villa at Beaulieu and visited the Villa Victoria, which belongs to Miss Alice Rothschild. He said it was packed—absolutely packed—with treasures. You must go there, *Belle-mère.*"

"I am not interested in treasures," Lady Rothley replied, "only in the Duke, and I hope I shall know the right things to say to him."

"He is very interested in paintings," Tempera said. "He has a magnificent collection at Chevingham House, as you must have seen, and some fabulous Old Masters in the country. Papa often spoke of the Chevingham Collection."

"If the Duke talks about them, what am I to answer?" Lady Rothley asked crossly. "You know I can never remember the names of all those tiresome painters. I get muddled between Raphael and Rubens. What is more, they all look the same to me."

"Then say nothing," Tempera begged. "When Papa lectured to students he told them that all he wanted them to do was 'to look and listen.' That is what you will have to do, *Belle-mère,* just look and listen."

She smiled and her voice softened as she added:

"You will look so beautiful doing it that there will really be no need for you to say anything."

"It is sometimes impossible not to," Lady Rothley replied, "and when they say to me: 'I know, of course, you like the style of Petronella, or Pepiana, or Popakatapettle,' or some such outlandish name, you will not be there to tell me who he really is."

She paused, and there was an alert look in her eyes.

"Tempera! Why not come with me?"

"What do you . . . mean?" Tempera enquired.

"I mean who is to know—who would ever know? No-one has ever seen you. You have never been anywhere and it would be everything to have you with me, to look after me and help me."

Tempera was very still. Then she said:

"Are you suggesting, *Belle-mère,* that I come with you as your lady's-maid?"

"Why not?" Lady Rothley asked. "I am sure the lady's-maids are well looked after. I know Arnold would have had plenty to say if she were not!"

Tempera did not reply and after a moment Lady Rothley said:

"Oh, for Heaven's sake, Tempera, you must see it is the only solution! You can look after my clothes, you can prime me as to which pictures are the best, although why anyone wants all those pictures on the walls I cannot imagine!"

"Supposing the Duke should discover that I was Papa's daughter?" Tempera said slowly. "Would he not think it very . . . strange?"

"How is he likely to discover it?" Lady Rothley asked. "You obviously will not travel in your own name, and I do not suppose for one moment that he has any idea that your father had a daughter—he has certainly never mentioned you."

Tempera rose to walk to the window.

She looked out at the grey sky and the drab, dirty little court-yard at the back of the house.

It had been a very cold, blustery March with

North winds and showers of sleet and hail, and she
was still shivering after driving back in the omnibus
from Trafalgar Square.

Only the brisk walk down Curzon Street had
swept away some of the cold, but her small nose felt
as if it did not belong to her and her fingers were still
icy.

She had a sudden vision of blue sea, of the flowers that her father had described to her, white Villas,
and the waves breaking against the rocks.

She turned round.

"I will come with you, *Belle-mère!* It will be an
exciting adventure, only we must be careful ... very
careful ... that we are not found out!"

                    *   *   *

As the hackney-carriage neared Victoria Station,
Tempera moved from the seat beside her Stepmother
to the narrow one opposite, with her back to the horses.

Looking at Lady Rothley, she thought she had
done a good job on the travelling-gown her Stepmother
had worn for some years, but which had now been
altered out of all recognition.

The deep blue of the skirt had been ornamented
with ruchings of silk in the same colour, and Tempera
had edged with the same material the jacket which her
Stepmother wore under her fur-lined cape.

The fur lining was an old one and had in fact
originally graced Sir Fancis's winter overcoat.

But it had been attached by Tempera's clever
fingers to her Stepmother's heavy plush travelling-cloak
and the least-worn parts made a wide collar which
framed her lovely face.

Tempera had turned herself out, on the other
hand, in what she thought was an exemplary manner
for a respectable maid-servant.

She wore a bonnet tied under her chin with ribbons, but which otherwise was a nondescript black.
The mourning she had been unable to discard since
her father's death now came in useful.

Her black gown was very severe, relieved of its

trimmings, and the cape which covered it was almost funereal in appearance.

She was not aware that it made her skin look almost dazzlingly white and brought out the red lights in her hair. In fact, she had been too busy to give herself more than a transitory thought in the last three days.

She had hardly slept as she shopped and sewed, pressed and ironed and packed for her Stepmother.

She only remonstrated with her once or twice, when the bills arrived for the gowns Lady Rothley had bought, totalling more than the fifty pounds which they had set aside for the excursion.

"We must have some cash with us," Lady Rothley had said the night before.

"I know," Tempera replied, "but you must be very careful, *Belle-mère,* very careful indeed, to spend as little as possible. We have already dipped into our nest-egg so that it is almost nonexistent."

"If I marry the Duke, the nest-egg will be of no importance whatever," Lady Rothley replied.

"And if you do not?" Tempera asked quietly.

Lady Rothley's beautiful face puckered like a child's.

"Do not be unkind to me, Tempera," she begged. "This gamble has to come off! I have to win—I have to!"

"Yes, I know, dearest," Tempera agreed, "but we must be sensible."

"How I hate being sensible!" Lady Rothley complained. "But I am sure the Duke will propose to me, and from that moment everything will be wonderful!"

She made a little sound of delight and went on:

"I will give a Ball for you at Chevingham House and we will invite all the most eligible young men in England. They will be all yours once I am out of the way!"

She was lost in one of her flights of fancy, which, Tempera knew only too well, usually had no substance in fact.

She could not help feeling apprehensively that perhaps the Duke had not intended anything more by his invitation than to ornament his party with a very beautiful woman.

From all Tempera had heard of the Duke of Chevingham, he was a very elusive young man who had evaded the match-making Mamas since he was nineteen.

At thirty, which Debrett told her he was now, there was no reason why he should wish to marry a widow, however beautiful, who was not his equal by blood or birth.

Tempera had the uncomfortable feeling that when it came to marriage, the great aristocrats, as they had done since the beginning of time, chose a suitable wife from amongst their equals.

It was therefore far more likely that the Duke of Chevingham would marry a daughter of the Duke of Northumberland, Devonshire, or Richmond, rather than Alaine Rothley.

But she knew it would only depress her Stepmother if she expressed such thoughts, so Tempera kept them to herself.

The hackney-carriage, never very swift at the best of times, was now slowly moving through the traffic round Victoria Station.

"Do not forget, *Belle-mère,* that from now on, even when we are alone, in case we are overheard, you must call me Riley."

"Of course I will try to remember," Lady Rothley said. "At least it begins with the same letter as your own surname."

Tempera smiled because her Stepmother was only repeating her own words.

It was always a mistake, she thought, to try to disguise one's self in too complicated a manner.

"Riley" was not too far removed from "Rothley." She had in fact chosen it because, as she had passed through the National Gallery to sell the drawing, she had noticed one of the magnificent portraits painted by Riley in the seventeenth century and remembered that there were no less than fifteen to be seen there.

The hackney-carriage drew up outside the station.

"I'll fetch a porter, M'Lady," Tempera said.

She stepped out first to beckon a porter and superintend the trunks which were to be taken down from the roof of the cab.

Lady Rothley alighted to stand looking helpless and very beautiful. Almost immediately a footman wearing the Chevingham livery came hurrying towards her.

He raised his cockaded top-hat from his head, bowed, and asked:

"Excuse me, Madam, but would you be with His Grace the Duke of Chevingham's party?"

"I am Lady Rothley!"

"Please follow me, M'Lady," the footman requested. "Your luggage will be attended to."

Another footman came to Tempera's side.

"Don't you worry," he said. "I'll see to this."

"Then be careful to leave nothing behind," Tempera admonished.

"Trust me," he said. "Here, give me that valise. There's no call for you to be lugging it about when we've got a porter."

He spoke in the familiar, easy manner of one servant to another, and when the luggage was finally piled upon the truck, Tempera walked beside him, following the porter into the station.

"Have you been South before?" the footman asked conversationally.

"No," Tempera answered. "I am looking forward to it."

"Nice to get away from the cold. I envies you."

"You are not coming?" Tempera asked.

"No such luck," he answered. "There's mostly 'froggies' in His Grace's Château. Permanent staff, so to speak. But of course Mr. Bates the Butler goes. He travelled with His Grace last night—and 'is valets. I wish I was one o' them!"

"Are you saying that His Grace has left already?"

"That's right," the footman replied. "He don't like
a lot of chatter and noise when he's travelling, and
who can blame him?"

He grinned at Tempera and said:

"Mind as 'ow you takes care of yourself with all
them amorous 'froggies' round. From all I 'ears, they're
not to be trusted with a pretty woman."

"I assure you I can take care of myself," Tempera
said primly.

"I hopes so," the footman replied, "but keep yer
eyes skinned, and don't go walking alone in the moonlight."

"I will take your advice," Tempera answered de-
murely.

"The only exception being 'yours truly,'" the footman added. "I'll be a-looking out for you on your return. We might have a bit o' fun if your Lady comes to
stay with us in the country."

"I shall have to consider that very carefully,"
Tempera said, trying to keep from laughing.

She knew it was only because she was so young
that a footman should dare to be so impudent to a
superior servant.

She could not help being amused by what had
happened so far, and when she reached the train she
found that everything had been organised in a most
efficient manner.

The Duke, she learnt, had two private coaches
attached to the usual boat-train.

One of them accommodated his guests like Lady
Rothley, and the other was occupied by the personal
servants, a Courier, and footmen who travelled only as
far as Dover.

There was an inordinate amount of personal bag-
gage, besides two other lady's-maids.

Immediately Tempera entered the coach she realised that these would be her companions not only on
the journey but also at the Château.

In the hierarchy, etiquette, and protocol that

existed below-stairs, she knew that lady's-maids considered themselves a race apart from the ordinary servants and were on equal terms only with the heads of the different departments.

She had learnt many years ago that when her mother stayed with her father in the great houses, the senior lady's-maid who took her employer's precedence sat on the right of the Butler in the Servants' Hall and the Chief Valet on the right of the Housekeeper.

She had a quick glance at the two other maids in the railway carriage and realised they were both very much older than she, and, she was quite certain, of more importance.

She was to learn as the journey began that Lady Holcombe's maid was Miss Briggs and Lady Barnard's Miss Smith.

They apparently knew each other well, but there was obviously no love lost between them. Miss Briggs took precedence over Miss Smith, and they both relegated Tempera to a very subsidiary position.

She realised, however, that they were both pleased that she had not been to the South of France before, which enabled them to patronise her with their superior knowledge: she would be forced to rely on them for certain information which only they could impart.

As the train started, however, they became quite relaxed, accepting a glass of champagne from the footmen carrying it into the next compartment and expressing their preference for pâté de foie gras sandwiches rather than those made with caviar.

"I'll say one thing for His Grace," Miss Briggs remarked, as she accepted her second glass of champagne, "he does things in style. You'd hardly believe when we went to stay with the Marquis of Tenby last year that I was expected to travel Second Class in an ordinary compartment in which there was a stranger!"

She spoke with such indignation in her voice that Tempera found it hard to restrain herself from laughing.

"I hope you told your Lady what you thought of such treatment," Miss Smith remarked.

"In no uncertain terms!" Miss Briggs replied. "In fact, I had her almost crying when I said that owing to the discomfort of the journey I would find it impossible to press her gown before the important party she was to attend on the night of our arrival."

"That's the way to teach them!" Miss Smith said with satisfaction. "I don't see why we should put up with anything, considering as how it's impossible for our Ladies to do without us."

She realised that Tempera was listening wide-eyed.

"You're very young, Miss Riley," she said disparagingly. "I suppose you've not had much experience?"

"Not much," Tempera agreed.

"Well, let me give you a word of advice," Miss Smith said, "you stand up for your rights and insist on having them. There's them, even these days, as thinks as how anything'll do for servants, but in our position we can soon teach them they're wrong!"

"We can indeed!" Miss Briggs agreed with a faint smile. "But there'll be no discomfort at the Château Bellevue, that's one consolation for our having to make this tiresome journey."

"I've not stayed there before," Miss Smith remarked.

"There's every luxury," Miss Briggs said with satisfaction. "And I don't mind telling you, Miss Smith, I think it's due to the fact that the Duke's unmarried. I've always found there's far more comfort in a house where there's no nosy, bossy mistress."

"I agree with you," Miss Smith said. "But it's strange, seeing how handsome he is, that His Grace has never been caught—although there's been plenty who have tried, take my word for it!"

"You can't tell me anything about that," Miss Briggs remarked. "Last year there were two ladies in the party making a dead set for him. I've never seen anything like it. Even Mr. Bates, the Butler, said he was astonished and it surpassed anything he had seen in all his years!"

"But they didn't succeed?"

"I should hope not!" Miss Briggs answered. "If you ask me, His Grace has no intention of marrying anybody. Dedicated to bachelorhood, that's what he is, and who shall blame him? With his looks and his money he can have any woman he wants without the trouble of giving her a wedding-ring."

"That's true enough," Miss Smith agreed.

The two women sniggered a little over their glasses of champagne and Tempera felt her heart sink.

If this was true, then the sale of the drawing and the money they had spent on her Stepmother's clothes had been for nothing!

Chapter Two

The journey across France even for the lady's-maids was more comfortable than Tempera had ever known or expected.

She had visited Paris when she was ten with her father and mother, and once after her mother's death her father had taken her with him to Brussels when he had no wish to leave her alone in London.

Otherwise she had little or no experience, but she had thought of French trains as noisy and uncomfortable.

It was quite different to be travelling in the Duke's private coaches, which consisted not only of a Drawing-Room and Dining and Sleeping cars for his guests, but also sleeping accommodation for the staff.

To Tempera's joy, she had a small compartment to herself, and very early in the morning she raised the blind from her window to look out on the passing countryside.

The fields in the sunshine were very beautiful, and then almost before she expected it there was the vivid blue of the Mediterranean as the train arrived at St. Raphael.

She would have been content to sit at the window for the rest of the journey, but she remembered her position, and, having enjoyed a cup of coffee and fresh *croissants* with the other lady's-maids, she moved with them into the sleeping car to attend to their mistresses.

Tempera had seen the Drawing-Room last night when she had unpacked for her Stepmother. The walls were hung with silk and the chairs and sofa were covered in pale green brocade.

The curtains were green and white, and a colourful Indian carpet covered the floor.

She was much impressed by it and also with the bed-room occupied by Lady Rothley, which was larger and more impressive than usual sleeping compartments.

Dark red Moroccan leather covered the washstand and the basin, which were made, as were all the items in the toilet service, of white metal.

Even in the morning, Tempera thought as she entered, Lady Rothley looked beautiful.

Her eyes were sleepy, but her golden-red hair hung over her plump shoulders, and Tempera thought that any man who looked at her would find her extremely desirable.

"You woke me up!" Lady Rothley said reproachfully.

"I am sorry, *Belle-mère,* but we shall arrive in about an hour, and you know how long you take to dress."

Then, realising that she had spoken without thinking, Tempera said quickly:

"You must get up, M'Lady. The train will not wait for long at Villefranche, where we alight before it goes on to Monte Carlo."

"We can talk ordinarily," Lady Rothley said. "I cannot believe anyone is listening at the key-hole."

"One never knows," Tempera replied, "and you must get in the way of addressing me as Riley."

"I am sleepy," Lady Rothley complained. "I can never sleep well in a train."

This Tempera was sure was untrue, but she was not prepared to argue.

She herself had been so entranced with the scenery she had seen since the train left St. Raphael that it was hard to think of anything but the beauty which had taken her breath away.

Her father had described it often enough, but that was very different from seeing it for herself.

She had resented the hours of darkness when she had been unable to see the land of France or the foot-hills of the Alps.

It was quite difficult now to get Lady Rothley out of bed and into the elegant pale-blue gown in which they had decided she should arrive.

As Tempera packed away her Stepmother's trav-elling-dress and fur-lined cloak and brought out a shady hat trimmed with cornflowers which matched her gown, she felt as if she were packing away the diffi-culties and problems of the past and opening the door to something new.

The train stopped at Nice for quite a time and Tempera longed to be able to explore the town of which Smollett had written, and the Promenade des Anglais, where her father told her the roués sat scrutinising the ladies with experienced eyes as they walked past.

But there was little time for reflection, because Lady Rothley was only just ready when the train, only a few minutes after leaving Nice, steamed into Ville-franche.

It was then that Tempera was to see the efficiency and the well-planned organisation with which the Duke surrounded his guests.

There were two carriages to convey them and a landau for the staff.

This had seats facing each other behind the horses, but it had also—a considerate touch—a linen canopy with a fringe to protect the occupants from the sun.

There were other vehicles to convey the mountain of luggage which the Duke's guests had brought with them, but before this was sorted out and identified by their personal servants the ladies and gentlemen had left in the carriages, Lady Rothley looking very lovely, her face shaded by a blue sun-shade which matched her gown.

When finally the landau set off and Tempera had made sure that every leather trunk and round hat-box belonging to her Stepmother was safely deposited in the baggage-wagon, she had time to look round her.

She had a glimpse of the port of Villefranche filled with high-masted merchant ships and gleaming white steam-yachts.

She imagined that one of them would belong to the Duke; but she did not like to appear inquisitive by asking questions and contented herself with enjoying the semi-tropical vegetation as the horses drawing them began to climb a hill.

There were olive groves, palm trees, and lovely dells bright with wild flowers on either side of the road.

Although Tempera was disappointed that they were not driving along the shore, she was delighted when between the trees she could see views of snow-capped mountains far away in the distance.

The maids were gossiping and at any other time Tempera would have listened to them, feeling she might learn something which could be useful.

But now she could only look at the wild orchids and yellow fritillaries, the white and violet crocuses, purple soldanellas, and other alpine flowers.

They travelled higher and higher until suddenly ahead of them, high above the sea and a promontory which Tempera was certain was St. Hospice, she saw silhouetted against the blue sky what appeared to be a Castle.

"What is that?" she asked the maid next to her.

Miss Briggs interrupted her conversation to glance up indifferently.

"That's Château Bellevue, where we're going."

"Is that the Duke's house?" Tempera asked in amazement.

"Impressive, isn't it?" Miss Briggs remarked.

It certainly was that and a great deal more.

It looked so like a mediaeval Castle standing sentinel over the whole countryside that Tempera expected it to be a modernised fortress.

But she found in fact that it had been built by the Duke's father at the beginning of the 1880s, at the same time that the Prime Minister, the Marquess of Salisbury, was building his Villa.

Perhaps determined to out-do everyone else, the sixth Duke of Chevingham had employed an Italian architect who had copied one of the famous Castles in Italy.

Together he and the Duke had chosen as a situation the most commanding site along the whole coast.

Perched on the very top of the cliff overlooking the small village of Beaulieu and the promontory of St. Hospice, on one side of the Château Bellevue there was a sheer drop of a thousand feet.

It looked almost as if it stood on the very brink of disaster and that a high wind might blow it down the steep rocks to destruction.

But it was very secure on the other side. Here the windows looked out over the valley and further heights to where far away in the distance there was a glimpse of mountain peaks.

The gardens running along the top of the cliff and descending behind the Château were, Tempera was to learn later, some of the most exotic and certainly the most exquisite in the whole neighbourhood.

Her first impression, as they rode through an arched gateway, was of a profusion of colour which made her heart leap.

Never had she imagined that bougainvillaea could be so glowingly purple or that climbing scented geraniums could show so many shades of pink.

The flicker of sunlight and shadow playing upon the walls had a beauty which she knew would have thrilled her father, and she had later only to look out one of the windows facing towards the sea to be spellbound by the vista below her.

On her arrival she had to concern herself with

finding her Stepmother's bed-room and being ready to receive and unpack the luggage as soon as it appeared.

Lady Rothley joined her soon after she started unpacking.

"It is so thrilling, Tempera!" she said as soon as the door was firmly closed. "There is a very small party and I am obviously paired with the Duke."

There was a note of excitement in her voice as she continued:

"There is only one unattached man, Lord Eustace Yate, who is already here. I have met him before and will do my best to keep out of his way."

"Why?" Tempera asked.

She was shaking out a gown which had become most unfortunately creased despite the fact that she had packed it very carefully in layer upon layer of tissue paper.

"Lord Eustace is the son of the Duke of Tring, who has to live out of England because he is an undischarged bankrupt," Lady Rothley explained.

"If Lord Eustace has no money, then we are certainly not interested in him," Tempera said.

"That is what I am telling you," Lady Rothley answered, "but he is rather attractive and has 'a way' with him, as my Nurse used to say."

"If he is impoverished like his father, he will not be interested in you," Tempera said.

"Not seriously, of course," Lady Rothley agreed. "He is looking out for a rich wife, we all know that, but he is going to find it difficult to find one."

"Why?" Tempera enquired as she pulled out another gown and realised with relief that it needed very little doing to it.

"Because," Lady Rothley explained, "word has got round that he is a ne'er-do-well, and no father of any consequence would allow his daughter to marry Lord Eustace, who will not even come into the title since he has an older brother."

She rested her face on her hands as she said reflectively:

"I think the Duke has asked him out of kindness. So that leaves me to pair with His Grace, while the others are all husbands and wives."

"There is plenty of room for more people in this enormous Château," Tempera remarked.

"That is what makes it so obvious that the Duke has invited me because he seeks my company," Lady Rothley said complacently.

She got up to look at herself in the mirror and said impatiently:

"For goodness' sake, Tempera, do something with my hair! I am going downstairs to join the Duke on the terrace and I look a wreck after such a sleepless night."

She looked nothing of the sort, as they both well knew, but Tempera rearranged her hair and Lady Rothley applied a discreet amount of powder to her pink and white skin and just a touch of red lip-salve to her mouth.

"Not too much!" Tempera said warningly.

"We are in France now," her Stepmother replied, "and the French women are heavily made up."

"I am sure they look very fast, and that is something you must avoid as an English Lady," Tempera said.

To herself she was thinking that it would be disastrous if the Duke's intentions towards her beautiful Stepmother were not honourable, but in fact something very different.

The more she saw of the Duke's possessions and the more she learnt about him made her feel despairingly that it was very unlikely he was considering marriage.

Unless of course he had been swept off his feet as her father had been and was in fact crazily in love.

There was however no point, she thought, in letting her fears upset her Stepmother, and there was no doubt as Lady Rothley turned from the mirror to go downstairs to the terrace that she was looking extremely beautiful.

"Do not forget to 'look and listen,' *Belle-mère*,"

Tempera said hastily before she opened the door. "Do not make any comments about the pictures except to say they are wonderful, until I have seen them first and tell you what to say."

"I will remember," Lady Rothley replied obediently.

"You can admire the Villa and the view, but the less you actually say the better," Tempera went on. "Just fix your eyes adoringly on the Duke. There are very few men who can resist that!"

"He should be fixing his eyes on me!" Lady Rothley retorted.

"I know that," Tempera said, "but remember, he is a Duke and they are a race apart from other men."

"They must still have a heart somewhere under the strawberry leaves," Lady Rothley replied with an unexpected sense of humour.

With a smile she was gone and Tempera went back to the unpacking. But she could not help feeling apprehensive.

Everything rested on the Duke finding her Stepmother compellingly alluring, but nobody knew better than Tempera how stupid she could be when it came to any intelligent conversation.

Then she told herself that perhaps she was unduly anxious.

It was the old Duke who had made the Chevingham Collection. Perhaps his son was not interested in the treasures that hung on his walls or filled the rooms in his enormous houses.

Ever since Lady Rothley had talked about the Duke, Tempera had been trying to remember what her father had said about him. But as far as she knew he had never met him.

She remembered his visiting Chevingham House and when he had come home he had told her mother and herself of the outstanding collection of Van Dykes which hung in one room and many other superlative Dutch Masters in another.

But his contact had been with the old Duke, and

the present owner of Chevingham House had come
into the title only four years previously.

Tempera of course had looked him up in Debrett.

It told her very little except his age and his names.

One of them, she was amused to find, was Velde,
and she thought that the old Duke must have chris-
tened his son after the name of the famous Dutch
Marine Artist because he had so many of his paintings
in his possession.

There had been, she remembered, no less than
three Van de Veldes, and she wished after learning the
Duke's name that she had time to seek out the pictures.

A number of those painted by Wilhelm Van de
Velde the Elder, not in oils but with a reed-pen on a
painted white background, were in the National Mari-
time Museum at Greenwich.

She told herself that this was important only if
the Duke had the same tastes as his father. If he had,
he would expect his wife to be as interested in pictures
as he was himself.

Tempera sighed.

It was almost impossible to make her Stepmother
understand paintings or remember for more than two
minutes at a time the name of the Artists, let alone
be able to recognise their work.

When she had first married Sir Francis and was
anxious to please him, Lady Rothley had allowed Tempera to take her to the National Gallery. But after half
an hour she had sunk down on a seat and refused to go
any farther.

"It is no use, Tempera," she had said, "I shall
never be able to tell one picture from another, and
quite frankly they bore me! All those smug faces, flat
landscapes, and naked goddesses give me indigestion!
Your father wants to think me beautiful and for me
to admire him. He does not care about anything else."

Tempera had to admit that this was the truth and
she had given up trying to educate her Stepmother.

Now she thought it was a pity that she had not

persevered, and she could only pray that the Duke would not realise how ignorant she was.

"I must find my way downstairs," she planned, "and try to look at the pictures myself. If I can tell *Belle-mère* a little about one, she can impress the Duke with her knowledge and forget the rest."

But it was not easy.

She found that the household, admirably organised by Colonel Anstruther, ran on very much the same lines as the houses in England, with the exception that all the servants, except the Butler, the valets, and the Duke's special footmen, whom they had brought with them, were French.

Because Colonel Anstruther had learnt by bitter experience that the two nationalities did not work well together, the French were kept apart from what Tempera was sure they thought of as the "English intruders."

Further, Colonel Anstruther had arranged that the three lady's-maids should eat alone in a small Sitting-Room by themselves, while the English menservants used another.

This occasioned quite a lot of grumblings from Miss Briggs and Miss Smith, who enjoyed the company of the valets. Especially one of the Duke's valets who had a sense of humour and kept them informed about what was going on in the house-party.

Mr. Bates, the Butler, would never gossip, Tempera learnt. He considered himself above the chitter-chatter of the other servants and moved about the Château like a pontifical Bishop.

He kept everybody in order and was in fact so awe-inspiring that even the French were impressed by him.

Tempera was therefore left to learn what was happening from Miss Briggs and Miss Smith.

They were undoubtedly extremely out-spoken and Tempera was soon aware that Lady Rothley had not exaggerated where Lord Eustace Yate was concerned.

"He was pursuing Lady Massingham's daughter last year," Miss Briggs announced. "But Her Ladyship

soon realised what was going on and whisked her
daughter away North and married her off to the Earl of
Hincham."

"He'll have to take an American," Miss Smith
said in the voice of one who proclaimed doom.

Miss Briggs laughed.

"You don't think an American with any real
money would fall for Lord Eustace, do you? Poeple
like the Vanderbilts expect no less than a Duke in return for their millions."

This, Tempera realised, was true, remembering
that May Goelet, whose father was reported to be the
richest man in New York, had married the Duke of
Roxburghe the previous year.

Another American, Helen Zimmerman, had become the Duchess of Manchester in 1900, and Con-
suela Vanderbilt the Duchess of Marlborough four
years earlier.

She had only been interested in these marriages
because the newspapers and magazines described the
priceless pictures owned by the bridegrooms.

They also revealed how many European treasures
had crossed the Atlantic purchased by the parents of
those three brides.

"American heiresses have the dollars," Miss
Briggs was saying, "but they wants their pound of flesh
in return for them."

Tempera began to feel quite sorry for Lord
Eustace, knowing only too well what it was like to be
without money.

She expected that he was trying, as she and her
Stepmother were, to keep up with the smart, spar-
kling set that circled round the Duke and had unlimited
millions to spend.

Even if Lord Holcombe's income could not be
compared with that of Sir William Barnard, the Hol-
combes certainly lived in style.

They had a large house in London, a country seat
in Hampshire, a Hunting Lodge in Leicester, and, Tempera heard, considerable Estates in Scotland.

Everything she learnt from the lady's-maids made her feel more and more depressingly sure that she and her Stepmother were asking too much in expecting an offer of marriage from the Duke.

She began to feel she had made a great mistake in not at the beginning discouraging Lady Rothley from setting her cap too high.

There must be other wealthy men who would find in her exactly what they longed for in a wife, and who would therefore be prepared to sacrifice their freedom, without condescending, as the Duke would be doing, to somebody far beneath him in Social rank.

But it was too late for second thoughts.

"The only thing I can do now," Tempera told herself, "is to go on hoping that by some miracle *Belle-mère* will pull it off."

Lady Rothley certainly seemed to glow with optimism when she came up to dress for dinner and she never looked more beautiful than when she sailed downstairs in a new gown by Lucille.

The following morning she could not wait to tell Tempera how much she had enjoyed the evening, how the Duke had paid her many compliments, and she had been put on his left at dinner.

"Tonight we are going to a party in Monte Carlo," she said, "and when I told him I did not know how to gamble he said he would teach me!"

Tempera gave a cry of horror.

"You cannot risk your own money, *Belle-mère.*"

"I have no intention of doing so," Lady Rothley answered. "I am not so stupid as you think! If I say I do not understand how to play, he will of course show me what to do, and if we lose he pays and if we win I keep the money."

There was sometimes, Tempera thought, quite a lot of shrewdness in her Stepmother's pretty head.

While she questioned the morals of such an attitude, she knew that in their case such an attitude was an absolute necessity.

Privately she made up her mind that she would

see that her Stepmother took none of her own money
with her in the small satin bag which matched her
gown, which she would carry with her.

"What are you going to do today?" she asked
aloud.

"We are going to steam along the coast in the
Duke's yacht," Lady Rothley answered, "have luncheon on board, and just 'peep' at the Casino. It was
Dottie Barnard who insisted on that. She is an inveterate gambler."

"Will you promise me on your word of honour
that you will not try to gamble unless you are with
the Duke?"

"Of course," Lady Rothley agreed. "But he will
be with us. We are going with him."

"Then that is all right," Tempera said with a sigh
of relief.

She felt like an anxious hen who was always worried when her chick was out of sight, but she knew she
could not trust her Stepmother not to do something
stupid just because she was too good-natured to say
"no."

She dressed her in one of the attractive thin
gowns which they had brought from London. At the
same time, she gave her a short close-fitting jacket to
put over it and insisted on her also taking a light cloak.

"It can often be very cold at sea," she said. "I remember Papa telling me that a storm can spring up in
the Mediterranean without any warning."

"If it does I shall lie down at once," Lady Rothley
said. "I hate the sea unless it is smooth."

"Do not tell the Duke so," Tempera begged. "I
am sure he enjoys yachting and would be bored with a
woman who was squeamish at the first sight of a wave."

"I am not as stupid as you seem to think, Tempera," Lady Rothley answered, with a sudden assump-
tion of dignity.

"Of course you are not," Tempera agreed.

She bent and kissed her Stepmother's cheek, and
Lady Rothley put her arms round her and hugged her.

"Thank goodness I have you here with me," she said. "It is so exciting that we can discuss things together, and I know I should make a thousand mistakes if you were not here to guide me."

"As soon as you have gone," Tempera said, "I am going downstairs to look at the pictures. To make it easy for me, *Belle-mère,* will you hide this handkerchief in one of the arm-chairs before leaving for the yacht? It will be the excuse I need if anyone finds me in the Gentry's part of the house."

"I will do that," Lady Rothley promised, "and when you choose a picture for me to talk about, for Heaven's sake find one painted by someone with an easy name to remember. You know how they all become tangled in my head!"

"I will find one," Tempera said confidently.

Carrying her white gloves, her hand-bag, her sunshade, and the handkerchief which Tempera gave her, Lady Rothley walked serenely down the stairs.

Tempera tidied away her Stepmother's things, arranged her silver brushes and combs on the dressing-table, and then because it was irresistible, went to the window.

She could see the port of Villefranche to the right and she wished she could be one of the party that was setting off towards Monte Carlo.

Tempera loved the sea and she was sure that unlike her Stepmother she would be a good sailor. She wondered if there would be any chance of her seeing the Duke's yacht and perhaps putting out to sea in it.

Then she told herself she was being greedy.

"It is so wonderful to be here, to be in the sunshine and to see the flowers after the cold of England. How could I be so ungrateful as to want more?"

There was nothing more she could do in the bedroom, and she thought that by this time the party would have left the Château and it was her opportunity to go downstairs.

She set off a little nervously, but she saw nobody as she went down the main staircase and entered the

Sitting-Room which her Stepmother had described to her as being "quite nice."

It was a great deal more than that.

It was very large, the walls were white, and so were the coverings on the furniture and the carpet.

It was quite unlike any room Tempera had ever seen before, and yet instinctively she knew both that it was right in its proportions with its huge windows looking out to sea and that it was a perfect setting for the pictures which were hung on the walls.

She glanced at them and was instantly entranced on seeing first an elaborate and colourful painting by Sebastino Ricci which seemed to glow with a brilliance that was only echoed by an enormous picture by Rubens on the adjacent wall.

There was a Poussin which Tempera liked, but she much preferred a delightful Bouchet of Madame Bergeret.

Her gown was painted in the manner of which he was a master, while the pink roses in the foreground seemed so real that one could almost pick them from the canvas.

Thrilled, Tempera walked from picture to picture. Then she realised that the Sitting-Room contained only very large ones, chosen, she thought, to make a great splash of colour against the white background.

Then she saw a door leading into another room and going through it she drew in her breath.

Here was a collection of small pictures that were after her own heart.

This room, she thought at a glance, must be the Duke's special Sanctum.

Again there were white walls and a white carpet, but there was an exquisite inlaid Regency desk with gold feet on which there lay a number of papers.

But it was the pictures which held Tempera's attention and there was such a profusion of them that it was hard to know where to begin to look.

The first one which attracted her was of St. George

and the Dragon, painted by the Sienese artist Giovanni Bazzi.

It was a picture about which her father had often spoken and which she had always longed to see.

The monstrous dragon was convulsively coiled back upon itself, while St. George thrust at it with his spear, his red cloak flying behind him against an exquisitely painted background of trees, Castles, ships, and sky.

"It is quite lovely!" Tempera exclaimed, thinking that she could go on looking at it forever.

Then she realised there was another *St. George and the Dragon* almost adjacent to it.

It was a small picture by Raphael, and again St. George, this time on a white horse, was piercing a writhing dragon while a lady he was rescuing knelt in prayer in the background.

'How Papa would have loved this!' Tempera thought.

Then next to it she saw a picture which she knew would have delighted her father more than anything else.

In fact she was sure he had talked to her about it when he had spoken so often of the painter Jan van Eyck.

It was a tiny painting entitled *Madonna in the Church,* and it was so exquisite in its miniaturesque manner that it was like a jewel.

The glittering sunlight reflected in warm bright patches on the stone floor, the faint breeze vibrating through the cool semi-darkness, and the sparkle of the precious stones seemed to Tempera to belong to the world of the spirit.

She felt it stir something within her, delving down into the depths of her being to evoke a response that was a part of her very soul.

"It was lovely . . . quite unbelievably lovely!" she said aloud, and wondered if she could ever explain to her Stepmother what it meant.

No man, she thought, could possess anything so precious and priceless and not be moved by it.

"All van Eyck pictures," she remembered her father saying, "reflect extreme sensitivity, as do his portraits of men and women."

But this was more than sensitivity, it was spirituality, and Tempera knew she would gladly give everything she had ever possessed just to be able to look at it every day of her life.

She remembered how her father had told her that some of Jan van Eyck's paintings bore the inscription *Als Ik Kan,* written in his own hand.

These words referred to the Flemish proverb meaning: "As I can, but not as I would."

"Perhaps that is a motto for us all," Tempera reflected.

She stood looking at the painting for some time. Then as she turned to look at the others in the room she was suddenly still.

To her astonishment, on the wall facing the desk was a picture she recognised. It was in fact the angel from the painting *Virgin of the Rocks,* by Leonardo da Vinci.

It was her father who had said to her when he took her to the Louvre:

"I have often wondered, Tempera, of whom you reminded me, and now I know. That is how you will look when you are older."

He pointed to the angel in Leonardo's great Masterpiece and Tempera had followed his direction with surprised eyes.

Now she knew that she had in fact grown in the years very much more like the angel than she had been at that time. Yet she told herself humbly it was a very idealised portrait and she could not possibly aspire to such beauty.

But undoubtedly there was some resemblance in the heart-shaped face with its small pointed chin, in the dark auburn hair parted in the centre over an oval forehead, the large tender eyes, and the half-smiling lips.

There was something very delicate and ethereal in the softly rounded long neck and slim body which were in fact very like Tempera's.

"I wonder why the Duke has it," Tempera asked herself.

It was strange that in a room full of original world-famous pictures he should have a copy of one figure from Leonardo da Vinci's Masterpiece.

Tempera had first seen the *Virgin of the Rocks* in the Louvre, and there was a version of the same picture in the National Gallery.

She had often looked at it with interest, although her father had informed her that it was generally agreed that the authentic and original version was the one in France.

The angel in each version looked very much the same, except that in the Louvre painting the colours were brighter and lighter and conveyed a translucency which was missing in the National Gallery version.

'It is strange . . . very strange . . . that the Duke should hang it here,' Tempera thought.

She turned to look again at the picture by van Eyck and decided that this was the one she would describe to her Stepmother and try to put into her mouth the right words in which to express her appreciation.

She could always say to the Duke:

"Shall I tell you which of your pictures I like the best?" Tempera planned.

He would be surprised that she had chosen something so small and exquisite when she herself was so large and he thought of her as a goddess by Titian.

Rehearsing exactly what her Stepmother should say, Tempera went back upstairs, taking with her the handkerchief she had been pretending to look for.

At the same time, she was determined that every moment while she was in Château Bellevue she would find an excuse to look at the pictures, to see them, if possible, with her father's eyes, and to listen to what she thought they could tell her.

"All beauty talks," Sir Francis had said often enough. "All great pictures have something to say. Do not only look with your eyes, Tempera, but listen to what your senses tell you, to what your heart says and what you feel deep in your soul."

"That is what I must try to do now," Tempera said to herself, "for I shall not often have such a marvellous opportunity as this."

She and the other two lady's-maids ate in their Sitting-Room at noon.

There were both French and English dishes to choose from, and while Miss Briggs and Miss Smith sniffed at anything that was strange and unusual, Tempera enjoyed *mussels marinières* and the chicken cooked *à la Provençale* in a casserole.

"I intend to lie down," Miss Briggs said as the meal finished. "I never sleep when I'm travelling, and with all this unpacking I'm completely exhausted!"

"I have every intention of having a good snooze," Miss Smith agreed. "We'll be up until all hours to-night."

"Do you wait up until your Lady returns?" Tempera enquired.

"Of course!"

Both Miss Briggs and Miss Smith spoke at once and turned shocked faces towards her.

"You don't suppose that Her Ladyship could unbutton herself?" Miss Briggs asked scathingly. "And no good lady's-maid would allow a housemaid to interfere."

"I waited up until six in the morning almost every night last time I was here," Miss Smith said. "It was dawn before Her Ladyship came home. Ridiculous, I thought it was, at her age!"

Miss Briggs laughed.

"You won't get my Lady out of the Casino until she's lost every penny she's got on her, or they close the doors!"

"You must feel very tired the next day," Tempera said sympathetically.

"We do," Miss Smith said tartly, "and that's why, if you take my advice, Miss Riley, you'll sleep whenever you get the opportunity. One thing about this place, the beds are comfortable, if nothing else!"

"I want another chair in my room," Miss Briggs said, as if she was determined to find fault. "I've already asked one of the French maids for one, but she didn't understand what I was saying. I'll have to get Mr. Bates to speak to Colonel Anstruther. I don't intend to be uncomfortable."

Tempera thought with a smile that they would neither of them be that, and when they disappeared in the direction of their rooms she went to her own but not to sleep.

In her luggage she had included her paint-box and a small canvas that took up very little room.

She had enjoyed painting when her father was alive and he had encouraged her by paying for her to have lessons ever since she was old enough to hold a brush.

She had no illusions that she would ever be a great Artist, but she loved painting and she knew because she had studied the methods of so many great Masters that she could produce a pleasant and attractive picture.

She was determined that she would take back at least one memento of her time in the South of France, and putting on a wide-brimmed hat she slipped out a side door and set out to explore the garden.

She had never imagined that anything could be so beautiful or so exquisite, but she was to learn later that the old Duke, having been compelled by his doctors in his old age to live in the South of France, had ordered plants from all over the world.

There were azaleas from the Himalayas and lilies from the West Indies, orchids from Malaya, besides a profusion of English flowers. These, especially the roses, the pansies, and the aubrietia, became slightly over-blown and exotic in the semi-tropical climate.

As the gardens were built on the slope of a hill, it was easy to plan cascades pouring down from stone figures to fall into pools filled with water-lilies and goldfish and then to descend again into a water-garden circled with plants and ferns which had a strange beauty of their own.

There were dark cypress trees like sentinels to guard the way and quite unexpectedly there would be a marble statue glowing white against the darkness of the trees, evoking a memory of Ancient Greece.

Tempera found herself moving as if in a trance.

Occasionally she passed gardeners busy weeding or replanting. They murmured: *"Bonjour, M'mselle,"* and she answered them in their own language.

Then, when she was quite a long way from the Château, she found herself in a small flower-garden where there was a herbaceous border against a stone wall covered with clematis.

The flowers attracted the attention of the butterflies and bees and formed such a lovely picture that as Tempera sat down on a marble seat she felt as if she were transported into a world that only her father would have understood.

She looked at the flowers immediately opposite her and knew this was what she must paint.

There were several lilies in bloom and beside them were pink roses so full and luscious that they reminded her of her Stepmother.

With them were some delicate bell-shaped little flowers to which she could not put a name, but which had a fairy-like lightness.

Tempera opened her paint-box and squeezed out the paint she required, then picked up her brushes.

She would have liked to have an easel to hold the small canvas, but instead she held it on her knee.

Then she started to paint.

She started at the top of the picture with the lily, then working swiftly she added the roses, and afterwards a number of other flowers.

She remembered to put in, with those she finished, as the Masters of flower-paintings always did, the butterflies, the bees, and the occasional drop of dew on a velvet petal.

Intent on what she was doing, painting because she loved it, longing to convey onto her canvas some of the beauty she saw, she forgot everything, even the time.

She had pulled off her hat because the seat on which she was sitting was in the shade, and because it was very warm she loosened the tight neck of her severe gown so that she could feel freer to concentrate on her work.

It must have been three hours later, perhaps more, when she heard a voice beside her say:

"That is very good!"

She started and turned her head, so startled from her concentration that for a moment it was hard to remember where she was and who was likely to be speaking to her.

Then she saw a gentleman, tall, square-shouldered, and bare-headed in the sunshine, wearing a white suit and looking at her with a strange expression on his face.

He was exceedingly good-looking, and yet at the same time there was something about him that told her he was not the usual type of man she had met before or indeed had ever thought of meeting.

There was something unmistakably different, and yet she was not sure what it was.

She looked at him, finding it hard to speak, feeling as if he had drawn her back from the heights where she had been for a time almost immortal.

They looked at each other for a long moment before the gentleman said:

"Let me see what you have done, and of course in the manner of de Heem or Bosschaert."

"I would not . . . aspire so high," Tempera answered, wondering why it was hard to find her voice. "It is . . . 'as I can' . . . but not 'as I . . . would.'"

The words came instinctively to her lips because

van Eyck's exquisite picture was still in her mind. Then
she saw the surprise in the gentleman's expression and
suddenly remembered who she was supposed to be.

"I . . . I am sorry," she said in a low voice, "perhaps I should not be here."

"Who are you?"

"I . . . lady's-maid to Lady Rothley."

"Then you are also my guest," the gentleman said,
"and may I say I am delighted that you should wish to
paint my flowers."

Tempera's eyes widened.

So this was the Duke! The Duke—and she had not
realised it!

She rose to her feet and said a little incoherently:

"Again I must . . . beg Your Grace's pardon . . .
but I . . . did not . . . know who you . . . were."

"There is no reason why you should," the Duke
answered, "but surely, if I may say so without sound-
ing rude, yours is a somewhat unusual talent to find in
a lady's-maid?"

As he spoke he looked down at her painting, then
took it from her hands.

"I only paint to amuse myself, Your Grace."

Tempera shut up her paint-box as she spoke and
picked up her hat.

"It is certainly something you should continue to
do," the Duke said, "and may I say I am surprised
that you have chosen to immortalise my flowers. Most
Artists come here to paint the view."

"Flowers are of course . . . easier," Tempera said
with a faint smile.

"I suspect that is not the real reason why you
chose them," the Duke answered.

Tempera had no answer to this and after a moment she said:

"I . . . think, Your Grace . . . I should return to
the . . . Château. Her Ladyship may need me."

"Her Ladyship is still in Monte Carlo," the Duke
answered. "I returned alone because I dislike gambling.

So if you wish to continue with your picture there is no hurry."

"I think perhaps I should finish it another day," Tempera replied, "that is, if I am not . . . encroaching on Your Grace's kindness by coming here."

"My garden is yours," the Duke said with a slight gesture, "and may I ask when you finish this picture if I may buy it from you?"

"No!"

Tempera spoke almost sharply because she was so surprised at his request.

He raised his eye-brows as if he was taken aback by the tone of her voice, and she said hesitatingly:

"I am . . . very grateful for Your Grace's generous impulse, but I recognise my inadequacy as a painter . . . just as you are . . . well aware of it."

The Duke smiled as if he understood what she was trying to say.

"If you compare your work with the Master-pieces on my walls, then of course there is no equality," he said. "But because you have painted this in my garden and because I would like a picture of my own flow-ers, I would be glad to purchase it."

She looked away from him and after a moment he said in a different tone:

"Perhaps you will give it to me?"

Tempera did not answer and he added:

"Unless of course you intend it for someone dear to your heart?"

"No . . . there is no-one like that," Tempera said quickly.

"Then may I have it?" the Duke asked insistently.

She could not understand why he persisted in wanting her picture and after a moment she said:

"If . . . it pleases Your Grace."

"Then I am very grateful," the Duke said, "and perhaps I may ask you to paint another part of the garden."

Tempera shook her head.

"No?" he questioned. "But why?"

There was just the suspicion of a dimple at the corner of her mouth as Tempera answered:

"Because it is the only canvas I have, Your Grace, and I do . . . enjoy painting."

He looked at her as if to see if she was serious, then said:

"Are you telling me that you intended to wipe this off and start again?"

"Exactly!" Tempera said. "It is what I always do with my pictures, which is why I leave no incriminating evidence of my . . . inadequacies behind me."

"That is wrong—completely wrong!" the Duke exclaimed.

He handed her the canvas which he held in his hand.

"Here is your picture," he said, "and I shall see that you have the means with which to complete several more while you are staying in my house."

Tempera looked at him, not sure what she should say or do.

She could hardly believe there was anything reprehensible in accepting some canvasses from the Duke as a present, and yet the whole conversation was something which she was sure should not have occurred.

It was not at all in keeping with the part she was playing.

"May I tell you that while I am a Patron of many of the Arts and in fact considered something of an authority," the Duke said in an amused voice, "I think never before have I knowingly provided a blank canvas for an Artist."

"Then perhaps it is something Your Grace should . . . not do now," Tempera said.

"Why not?" he asked. "I ask only one thing in return for what you call my generosity, and that is that I may see your pictures when you have finished them."

"I would . . . much rather you did not . . . look at them."

"I want to look at them. I think you have a very unusual talent, Miss . . . ?"

He smiled.

"You have not told me your name."

"Tempera . . ." there was a little pause, "Riley."

"Tempera," he repeated. "That is unusual, as everything else about you is unusual. I am sure there is no need for me to tell you that Tempera paintings were characterised by a brilliance and luminosity unequalled by the use of other media."

"They are also less likely to crack than oil-paintings," Tempera said, "but one can never be quite sure of it!"

Even as she spoke she thought it was extremely stupid of her not to have thought of changing her Christian name.

Tempera was so obviously the sort of name that only an Artist would give his daughter and she had been extremely indiscreet in answering the Duke without really considering what she was saying.

The Duke laughed, then said reflectively:

"I have never before met anyone called Tempera. It is a delightful name and what I might have expected, Miss Riley, in someone as original as yourself."

"I have no wish to be anything but conformable and to look after Her Ladyship as she expects me to," Tempera said. "It has been a great privilege, Your Grace, for me to come to the South of France, and I hope that nothing I have said has seemed out of place or indeed . . . impertinent."

"I should think neither of those things could apply to you, Miss Riley," the Duke replied.

"Then I must thank Your Grace for the encouragement you have given me."

Tempera curtseyed as she spoke, turned, and walked away along the twisting path among the cypress trees which would lead her eventually up to the Château.

As she went she had the feeling that the Duke's eyes were following her and it was with difficulty that she forced herself not to look back.

Only when she was quite sure that she was out of sight did she ask herself how this could have happened.

How could she have spoken to the Duke of all people in such an easy, conversational manner?

If nothing else, he must have thought her a very strange lady's-maid, and that was something neither she nor her Stepmother wished him to think.

"I wish I had not come," Tempera said aloud.

She knew even as she spoke that she lied.

Chapter Three

By the time Tempera got back to the Château she felt her mind was in a whirl and it was difficult to think coherently.

How could she have talked to the Duke in such a manner, which, she felt, had been far too self-revealing?

Then she told herself there was no reason why he should connect her with her father, and after all it was possible for a lady's-maid, like other servants, to have a talent.

The thought was however not reassuring, and in the time that followed before Lady Rothley returned from Monte Carlo Tempera could only go over and over again her conversation with the Duke and wish that it had not happened.

He was undoubtedly the best-looking and the most attractive man she had ever seen, but, as she had thought at first sight, there was something else about him, something that she was sure would make him outstanding even in a room full of distinguished men.

Then she wondered if perhaps in her own mind she was associating him with his pictures and giving him an aura he did not really deserve.

It was his father who had made the collection, and it was to be expected that he should appreciate it. But that was not to say that he was on the same level as a

51

connoisseur and authority like her father, whose judge-
ment had been respected all over the world.

If the Duke was a real connoisseur, Tempera
tried to tell herself, he would not appreciate her ama-
teurish painting.

She looked at her unfinished canvas and knew
that, while it was quite good, it could not in any way
begin to emulate the Great Masters of flower-pictures
like Jan de Heem, whom the Duke had mentioned.

She could copy them to a certain extent, and her
brush-work, because she had been taught by experts,
was outstanding.

But she knew she had not the spark of genius
which her father would search for when he was shown
a painting so that he knew immediately whether it was
genuine or a fake.

"I am a fake," Tempera told herself, and thought
that was true in more than one way.

She was a fake painter and a fake lady's-maid. If
the Duke was perceptive he would be aware of that.

She felt herself tremble with sudden agitation.

If she had spoilt her Stepmother's chances of
marrying the Duke she would never forgive herself.

She walked up and down in Lady Rothley's bed-
room and for the first time since she had entered the
Château the view outside had no attraction for her.

All she was trying to find was some reasonable
explanation that her Stepmother could give if the
Duke mentioned her, which she was sure was inevitable.

When Lady Rothley returned she was flushed
and excited at how enjoyable the day had been.

"The Duke's yacht is fantastic!" she said. "It is
enormous, so comfortable, and Monte Carlo is all I
expected it to be. Oh, Tempera, I am enjoying myself!"

"The Duke came home alone."

"How do you know?" Lady Rothley enquired.
"He said he hated Monte Carlo and we left him on

the yacht. When we had finished visiting the Casino there were carriages waiting to bring us back."

Tempera drew in her breath.

"The Duke found me in the garden and spoke to me."

"Did he?" Lady Rothley asked, quite unperturbed. "Now you have seen how attractive he is! There was another most delightful man at the Casino who is coming here to stay tomorrow."

"I do not think you understand what I am trying to tell you, *Belle-mère*," Tempera said slowly. "The Duke found me painting and I am sure he will think it a very odd accomplishment in a lady's-maid."

"Why should you not paint if you want to?" Lady Rothley asked, studying her reflection in the mirror. "After all, lady's-maids embroider. I cannot see much difference between sewing and painting."

"I am afraid that because I am your maid he might somehow connect me with Papa."

"He has only mentioned your father once," Lady Rothley said, "and that was to say that his father the old Duke had a great admiration for him. As a matter of fact, I do not believe they ever met."

"No, I was thinking that might be so," Tempera said with a note of relief in her voice.

"It therefore follows he would not be interested in your father's daughter," Lady Rothley said. "Do not fuss, Tempera. If he thinks that you are interested in painting, it may make up for my deficiencies!"

She laughed as she spoke, but Tempera's face was serious.

"Do be sensible about this, *Belle-mère*," she begged. "The Duke will very likely mention it to you, and I have thought of what you must say."

"What is it?" Lady Rothley asked indifferently.

"You must say that you know very little about me . . . that I was recommended by a friend as you had to engage a lady's-maid in a hurry. Be very casual and say you are not even certain you will keep me."

"There is no doubt about that," Lady Rothley replied. "If I told the truth I should say that I could not manage without you!"

"Please, *Belle-mère,* listen to what I am saying," Tempera pleaded. "The Duke is bound to be curious, for I suppose I do look different from the average lady's-maid."

As she spoke she thought of the picture which her father had always thought she resembled hanging opposite the Duke's desk in the room downstairs.

Would he too think there was some resemblance?

Then Tempera told herself that this was too far-fetched even to consider.

Was it likely that he had even looked at her closely enough to compare her with a picture by one of the greatest Masters of painting the world had ever known?

She gave a sudden smile which lit up her face.

"You are right, *Belle-mère,*" she said. "I am making a mountain out of a mole-hill. Treat anything the Duke says about me very indifferently; and what I really wanted to tell you is . . ."

"The Count paid me the most exquisite compliments," Lady Rothley interrupted in a dreamy voice, and Tempera knew she had not been listening to anything she said.

"I have always thought that Italians have exquisite manners," she went on, "but they also make even the slightest flattery sound as if it came from the very depths of their hearts."

"*Belle-mère,* do listen to me! I want to tell you about a picture which you could talk about to the Duke. It is by Jan van Eyck, and I am sure you can remember his name. It is exquisite! Really exquisite!"

"That is the way the Count described me," Lady Rothley replied. "'You are exquisite!' he said. 'And the embodiment of sunlight!'"

Tempera tried again:

"You are not listening, *Belle-mère.*"

Lady Rothley rose from the stool in front of the dressing-table.

"I do not want to listen, Tempera. I am tired and I have a head-ache. You can tell me about your picture another time."

"But I want you to talk about it to the Duke this evening at dinner."

"We are not dining here. We are going to Monte Carlo to dine with Princess Daisy of Pless. I understand from Lady Holcombe it will be a very, very smart party, and I must wear my best gown."

Tempera gave up the hopeless task of trying to talk to her Stepmother.

'Perhaps it will be easier tomorrow,' she thought, and concentrated on helping Lady Rothley undress so that she could lie down for an hour before dinner.

As soon as Tempera's own evening meal was finished she went to her bed-room and taking out her paints started to finish the picture she had begun in the garden.

The outline of all the flowers she had chosen was there, while the lilies and the roses were finished. Fortunately, she had found replicas of the rest in the big vases of flowers which had been placed in her Stepmother's bed-room.

She brought one vase to her own room, set it down on her dressing-table, and sitting on the bed tried to transfer their texture and colour onto canvas.

She could understand why the Duke was surprised by the fact that she had not attempted to paint the view, but she had always loved flower-pictures.

It was one of her teachers who had encouraged her to specialise in flowers rather than attempt figures or landscapes.

She had an idea that he thought flowers were particularly feminine and therefore more appropriate for women, but she loved them for themselves.

Her mother had hung several of her first pictures in her bed-room.

"Surely those are saleable?" her Stepmother had asked when they were taking the pictures from the walls after her father's death.

"I am afraid not," Tempera answered, "and in the future they will be the only decoration we can afford."

"Well, I think they are very pretty," Lady Rothley said loyally, "far prettier than some of those pictures which belonged to your father."

Tempera had laughed and kissed her, but she had not taken it as a compliment, rather as a show of ignorance.

Now she looked at her own painting and remembered that the Duke had admired it.

"He was just being polite," she told herself.

But there was no reason why he should be polite to an unimportant and obscure female, even before he knew she was nothing but a servant staying in his Château.

'Perhaps I can make a little money by painting when we get back to London,' Tempera thought.

Then she realised she was already accepting defeat where her Stepmother's aspirations were concerned.

'Belle-mère is beautiful enough for the Duke,' her thoughts continued. 'It is just that I am sure he is intelligent and would want a woman who could talk to him intelligently.'

Yet she thought she was being pessimistic. After all, her father, who was an extremely clever man, had been happy enough with his second wife.

He had treated her rather like a child: there was no doubt that he had delighted in her beauty, but when his eyes were watching her Tempera had the idea that he closed his ears to anything she might be saying.

It was midnight before Tempera finished painting, and then she went along the quiet passage to her Stepmother's room.

"I shall be waiting up for you, Belle-mère," she had said. "After all, the other lady's-maids wait up for their mistresses and would be horrified if I did not do so."

"I was quite prepared to come to your room and

waken you so that you could undo my gown, as we have always done," Lady Rothley said. "But what you had better do, Tempera, is to lie down and sleep on my bed until I return."

"If anyone saw me committing such *lèse-majesté* they would have a fit!" Tempera replied.

"Lock the door," Lady Rothley replied. "I will knock gently if you are asleep when I get back, but if I talk loudly on the stairs it will wake you up."

Tempera kissed her.

"You are very kind and considerate, *Belle-mère*."

"Why should I not be?" Lady Rothley had answered. "You are extremely kind to me, Tempera, and you have just told me that I look beautiful tonight. I know it is because you have done my hair so skilfully."

There was no doubt that she had not been exaggerating.

Lady Rothley did in fact look breathtakingly beautiful, and more than ever like a Titian goddess.

"Have a lovely time," Tempera said, "and do not forget to concentrate on the Duke."

"If the Count is there I shall find it terribly hard not to listen to his compliments," Lady Rothley teased.

Then as she saw the expression on Tempera's face she added quickly:

"Do not worry, I am very conscious that I am the bait and the Duke is the fish we are after. He will not escape if I can help it!"

She laughed lightly and picking up her satin bag in which Tempera had put no money she went down the stairs.

Because she was uneasy—in fact, as she admitted to herself, very anxious—Tempera did lie down on the big double bed in her Stepmother's bed-room, but she found it impossible to sleep.

Instead she rose to pull back the satin curtains from the window and look out at the night.

There was a half-moon climbing up the sky and the stars were reflected in the smooth sea.

It was so lovely and she wondered why there were not a thousand painters trying to convey the scene on canvas.

Down below there were lights in the little village of Beaulieu and an occasional light amongst the green trees on the promontory of St. Hospice.

Far away to the right in Villefranche there were the lights of the yachts and ships anchored in the port.

'It is all so beautiful, so peaceful, and so quiet,' Tempera thought. 'It is a part of God, and why should my silly little problems matter? Doubtless they will solve themselves.'

She stood looking out at the sea for a long time.

When she went back to lie on the bed it was as if calming hands had been placed on her forehead and she instantly fell asleep.

* * *

In the morning when Tempera breakfasted with the two older maids they were both grumbling disagreeably about the late hour at which their Ladies had returned.

"It's always the same when we come to the South," Miss Briggs said snappily. "I'm thinking of saying to Her Ladyship if this continues I'll have to make a change."

Both Miss Smith and Tempera knew that this was unlikely as she had been with Lady Holcombe for twelve years and was undoubtedly set in her ways.

At the same time, Tempera could sympathise with them. She was quite certain that neither Miss Smith nor Miss Briggs would outrage convention by lying on their employers beds as she had done.

As her Stepmother had anticipated, she had awakened immediately at the sound of voices coming up the stairs and had been waiting to open the door before Lady Rothley reached the landing.

As her Stepmother had turned to say good-night to Lady Barnard and Lady Holcombe, Tempera had a glimpse of the gentlemen in the hall below.

There was no mistaking the Duke, she thought, who was taller than his friends, and he seemed to carry himself with an assurance which they lacked.

Then Lady Rothley had entered the bed-room and Tempera could see him no longer.

When she called her Stepmother it was late in the morning. Lady Rothley was sleepy but still elated with the success she had created the night before.

"Dozens of people complimented me," she said. "I do not mind telling you, Tempera, that I was a sensation—I know I was!"

"I am so glad, dearest, but do eat your breakfast while it is hot. The Chef was scandalised that any of the ladies should require an English breakfast, although he is used to cooking it for the gentlemen."

"I have just remembered something else," Lady Rothley said. "I won quite a lot of money last night."

"I will count it and see exactly how much you did gain," Tempera replied.

She knew her Stepmother was very vague about the French currency and because they were the same size had a way of believing that a franc equalled a sovereign.

"It is all in my satin bag," Lady Rothley said.

Tempera looked round the room.

"It is very remiss of me, but I cannot remember your having it with you last night. I suppose I should have noticed."

"Then if it is not here, I must have left it downstairs," Lady Rothley said. "I know I had it with me in the carriage because I felt it to make quite certain."

"Did you go into the Sitting-Room when you returned?" Tempera asked.

"Yes, the men drank champagne and I had a glass of lemonade."

"Then that is where you must have left it."

"Go and get it quickly," Lady Rothley cried. "It would be disastrous if one of the servants stole it."

"I think that is unlikely," Tempera answered. "I

gather the French staff have been here for years and
Colonel Anstruther trusts them completely."

She was sure there would be no petty thieving in
a house that was filled with treasures worth thousands
of pounds. But because her Stepmother looked worried she went downstairs to the Sitting-Room, hoping
she would not encounter the Duke.

There was nobody about and she thought that
the guests who had already risen would be out on the
terrace which was built on one side of the Château
and not directly in front of the main windows.

Then as she found her Stepmother's bag lying
on a small Sheraton table beside the sofa she heard
someone come into the room behind her.

She turned round, somehow expecting to see the
Duke, but saw instead another gentleman who was also
good-looking, but very different from the man she had
expected to see.

He looked at her and smiled, and it made him
seem attractive.

"Who are you?" he asked. "I do not seem to have
seen you before."

Tempera dropped him a respectful curtsey.

"I am lady's-maid to Lady Rothley, M'Lord."

As she spoke she realised that this must be Lord
Eustace Yate.

She had seen both the other gentlemen in the
party when they were at Victoria Station, and again
when they left the train at Villefranche.

Miss Briggs and Miss Smith had told her the
truth about Lord Eustace. He was good-looking, and
yet there was something raffish about his appearance that undoubtedly revealed his character.

"A lady's-maid—and a very pretty one!" he said
in a manner which Tempera immediately resented.

Holding her Stepmother's bag in her hand, she
walked towards the door, but although he seemed hardly to move Lord Eustace blocked her way.

"No hurry," he said. "I would like you to tell me
something about yourself. How many young men have

you, and do you enjoy the warmth of the Mediterranean?"

"Very much, thank you, M'Lord," Tempera said coldly. "And now, if you will excuse me, Her Ladyship is waiting."

"Her Ladyship can wait!" Lord Eustace retorted. "I find you as delectable to look at as your mistress. Does that surprise you?"

Tempera thought he moved a little nearer to her and now she straightened herself until her eyes were almost level with his. Then she said slowly:

"It does not surprise me, M'Lord. It is entirely in keeping with what I have already heard about Your Lordship."

She saw the astonishment in his face, and quickly, before he could prevent her, she moved round him and reached the door.

As she hurried upstairs she heard him laugh.

"Here is your bag," she said as she entered her Stepmother's bed-room, "but I met Lord Eustace in the Sitting-Room. You will do well to avoid him, *Belle-mère*. He is a bad lot, as the other maids have told me he is."

"Of course, everybody knows that," Lady Rothley said. "At the same time, he is witty and amusing, and Sir William, for all his money, is a dead bore!"

Tempera smiled.

"One cannot have everything in life."

"No," Lady Rothley agreed. "But I do not mind telling you, Tempera, I find the Duke rather difficult to talk to."

Tempera sat down on the edge of the bed.

"Belle-mère, I want you to listen to me about this picture."

Lady Rothley gave a little cry and put her hands over her ears.

"I do not want to hear about pictures," she said peevishly, almost like a spoilt child. "I want to tell you about myself and the compliments that were paid to me last night. Do you know what the Count said?"

Tempera got down from the bed.

"I do not want to hear about the Count," she replied, "nor about any other man you may meet in Monte Carlo. You came here for one reason, and one reason only, *Belle-mère,* and you know we have spent all our money."

"Now you are being unkind to me," Lady Rothley pouted. "See how many francs I won. At one time it was much more, but the Duke would not go on playing."

It was no use being cross, Tempera thought, and whatever she might say her Stepmother would still be herself, and because she was so beautiful, Tempera could only hope she would get away with it.

The francs which filled her small satin bag came to about fifteen pounds. Although it was not an astronomical sum, it was at least a useful contribution to their diminished funds, Tempera thought, as she put it away carefully in a safe place.

"What are you doing today?" she asked, having prepared her Stepmother's bath.

"We are lunching at the Rothschild Villa . . ." Lady Rothley began to say, but was interrupted by Tempera giving a cry of delight.

"Oh, *Belle-mère,* I am so thrilled that you are going there! Please, for my sake, look at everything so that you can tell me about it. Papa could talk of nothing else when he returned home and he even showed me reproductions of some of their pictures and marvellous French furniture."

She gave a little sigh.

"He told me too about Waddesdon, the house which the Rothschilds built in Buckinghamshire. There is a magnificent . . ."

She stopped.

There was no point in going on because she knew that her Stepmother was not listening. Then she said:

"I will tell you a story that will amuse you, *Belle-mère.* It will remind you to compliment Miss Alice Rothschild on her garden."

Lady Rothley looked slightly bored, but Tempera continued:

"It was when Queen Victoria visited the Villa. As a surprise, Miss Alice Rothschild ordered a mountain road to be levelled and widened! Can you believe it? It was done in three days! It meant building up walls, picking up huge stones, covering the small ones with macadam, and diverting a stream!"

She thought she had her Stepmother's attention and continued:

"But when Queen Victoria was admiring the garden she walked on a newly planted flower-bed. Miss Rothschild was outraged. 'Come off at once!' she exploded."

"Was the Queen angry?" Lady Rothley enquired.

"No," Tempera replied. "She did as she was told, but afterwards the Queen always referred to Alice Rothschild as 'the All-Powerful'!"

"I think that is a funny story," Lady Rothley said, who was always intrigued by social anecdotes. "I wonder if the Duke knows it."

"I expect so," Tempera said, "but if he tells you, pretend you have not heard it before."

By the time her Stepmother was dressed and a footman had knocked on the door to say the carriage was waiting, it was well after twelve o'clock, when Tempera was expected to have luncheon with the other maids.

When she joined them they had nearly finished and were in a hurry to get to their own rooms to lie down.

Thankfully she finished her own meal in peace and quiet, enjoying the ripe cheese, which Miss Briggs thought "disgusting," and the salad, which neither she nor Miss Smith would touch.

'There is no-one in the world more set in their ways or more prejudiced than British servants,' Tempera thought with a smile, and wished she could have laughed about it with her father.

She thought that what she missed most was his sense of humour.

He would always see the funny side of any situation, however disastrous, and he told her many times of various *faux pas* that had been made in houses like the Rothschilds' where people pretended to be more knowledgeable than they were.

She walked into her small bed-room and saw at once that there was a large parcel on the bed.

She knew what it was, and opening it was not surprised to find half a dozen canvasses.

They were all small but beautifully mounted and of the very finest material.

"So the Duke did not forget,' she thought.

She remembered a little apprehensively that his condition had been that he should see the pictures she painted.

She had thought last night that the one she had already painted was finished, but when she took it to the window she could see a dozen details that might have been more skilfully executed.

"I will go back at the same time to where I was yesterday," she told herself, "to make quite certain the light is right."

There could be no question today of her being interrupted by the Duke, for he had gone with his party to luncheon at the Villa Victoria, which Miss Rothschild had named after the Queen.

Tempera was quite certain the meal would be long-drawn-out over the superlative food for which the Rothschilds were renowned.

'I am safe,' she thought. 'If the Duke is to see this picture, it must be right.'

She picked up her large-brimmed hat and hurried down through the gardens, too intent on her mission to stop, as she had done yesterday, to watch the cascading water or look at the distant snow-capped mountains or the water-garden.

The flowers she had chosen to paint were now fully blown, but she thought she could improve on the translucency of the lily and make the roses look a richer pink.

"Perhaps I am over-painting," she worried a little later, remembering that her father had always said it was a lamentable error into which many Artists fell.

Then she shrugged her shoulders and told herself that without doubt the Duke would only glance at her picture and consign it to the waste-paper basket.

Deliberately she forced herself not to continue touching up the flowers, but to leave them as they were. Then she walked back towards the Château, enjoying the garden as she had not been able to do before.

It was so lovely, so perfect, that she could not understand why anybody should wish to go elsewhere when they owned this oasis of perfection.

Then she told herself there were quite a lot of things she should be doing for her Stepmother and she had spent enough time enjoying herself.

She walked back into the house.

Everything was very quiet, in fact the only sound she could hear was the buzz of the bees on the flowers climbing over the terrace.

Everyone, Tempera thought, would be having a siesta, even Colonel Anstruther.

Fortified by the conviction, she walked into the Sitting-Room and through the other door into the Duke's Study.

She put her painting down on the desk, and then as a thought struck her she picked up one of his pencils.

On the back of the picture she wrote the Flemish proverb used by Jan van Eyck:

"Als Ik Kan."

He would understand that it was the best she could do.

She was well aware how humble and inadequate it must look in a room embellished by some of the greatest Masterpieces in the world.

Having set the canvas where the Duke could not

fail to see it, she looked first at the picture *Madonna in the Church* and thought it was even more lovely than she remembered.

Near it she found an exquisite little oil-painting by Petrus Cristus. It was only ten inches by eight and a half, a portrait of a young girl, and Tempera remembered that he was thought to have been a pupil of Jan van Eyck.

There were so many other pictures she wanted to examine but she felt that time was passing and she had no intention of being found by Colonel Anstruther or anyone else in what she was sure was the Duke's private room.

She took one last look at the portrait of the angel.

"If I really looked like that I should be very, very proud," she said beneath her breath.

She turned towards the door, but as she did so she had a sudden impulse to take her own painting away with her.

Suppose the Duke showed it to other members of the house-party? Suppose he held her up to ridicule about it? Suppose he talked and the other servants heard about it and they thought she was trying to draw attention to herself?

Suddenly she thought she had been very stupid.

She picked up the small canvas and holding it closely against her breast ran through the Sitting-Room and up the stairs to her own bed-room.

She looked at the empty canvasses waiting for her and knew she had no right to accept them and still less right to be involved with the Duke.

This was the last thing that should happen; and if he thought she had gone back on her word, what did it matter?

He would forget her and that was the best thing that could happen!

Deliberately Tempera put the new canvasses in a cupboard so that the housemaid who did her room would not see them, then she lay down on her bed and closed her eyes.

Despite the fact that she had slept for several hours before her Stepmother returned, she was in fact tired and she drifted into a state that was half-dreaming, half-reality. . . .

She awoke with a start to be aware that whether it was a dream or a thought it had been of the Duke.

"You are becoming obsessed with the man," she told herself sharply. "Just remember, the only person of importance is *Belle-mère,* and it is not going to help her if the Duke continues to think about painting.

"I have behaved very stupidly," Tempera accused herself.

When her Stepmother returned she tried to make up for what she thought of as her deficiencies by being particularly attentive.

All Lady Rothley wanted, however, was someone to listen to the compliments she had received at the Rothschild party, and only after she had repeated word for word all that had been said did Tempera ask eagerly:

"What did you think of the Villa? Was it very fine?"

She knew that her Stepmother forced herself to concentrate on what she had seen.

"It was rather overcrowded," she said, "and very rich, rather like a surfeit of pâté de foie gras."

Tempera laughed.

"You are quoting someone else. You did not think of that yourself!"

Lady Rothley smiled.

"It was the Duke, as a matter of fact. It is what he said as we were driving home. Then Lord Eustace looked at me and said meaningfully:

" 'Some pâtés are so delicious that one can never have enough of them!' "

It was hopeless, Tempera thought, to try to get any further impressions from her Stepmother, and there was no use in plaguing her.

Instead, she listened to all the gossip that Lady Rothley had accumulated about the distinguished people staying in the vicinity and in Monte Carlo, until it was time for her to rest.

"There is another party tonight," she yawned, "and I suppose we shall not be back until dawn, because wherever we dine we always go afterwards to the Casino."

Her eyes brightened as she added:

"Perhaps I shall win again."

"You are not to play unless the Duke plays with you," Tempera said quickly.

"There are other gentlemen who are even richer."

"We are not concerned with them," Tempera replied in a hard voice. "Whatever you do, *Belle-mère*, keep beside the Duke and remember that the men who pay you these compliments will remain here when we have returned to London."

"I have not forgotten," Lady Rothley promised lightly, "but, Tempera, it is so wonderful to be made a fuss of, to know that men are looking at me with that 'swimmy' expression in their eyes and that they are longing to touch me."

She threw herself back against the pillows and said:

"There are times when I really feel quite passionate, which is something that has never troubled me before."

"Then concentrate it on the Duke," Tempera said.

She pulled the curtains over the open windows as she spoke.

"Try to sleep, dearest," she said as she walked towards the door.

"I shall, after all that food and drink at luncheon," Lady Rothley yawned. "It was delicious but it has made me very sleepy."

Tempera shut the door quietly and she was thinking as she walked towards her own bed-room that if her Stepmother continued to eat and drink so much, her new gowns would soon need letting out.

But it was impossible to find fault when Lady

Rothley was ready to go out to dinner in another new gown, looking as if she had stepped straight out of a Titian picture.

Her white shoulders were framed in tulle, and her waist, tightly laced by Tempera, seemed almost to divide her anatomy in the approved manner.

Tempera had already learnt from Miss Briggs and Miss Smith that the ladies were exceedingly jealous of Lady Rothley, especially Lady Holcombe.

She was considered a beauty, but her red hair and slanting green eyes were completely eclipsed by Lady Rothley's shining brilliance.

"Try to rest as you did last night," Lady Rothley said affectionately before she left her bed-room. "I feel it is very selfish of me to make you stay up so late, but I will make it up to you, dearest Tempera, when I am a Duchess."

"Cross your fingers!" Tempera laughed. "You know it is unlucky to boast."

Lady Rothley kissed her Stepdaughter and Tempera tidied the room, took the things she had to wash, then went to her own supper.

The two elderly maids were more disagreeable than usual.

"It's getting too hot for me," grumbled Miss Smith. "As I said to Her Ladyship this morning, it's too late in the year to be coming to the South. We should have come soon after Christmas when those winds were biting into us and the Castle was my idea of hell!"

"I rather enjoy the heat," Miss Briggs said, "but only if I don't have to work. The mere idea of a hot iron makes me shudder!"

Miss Smith leant confidentially across the table.

"I understand that for a few centimes there's a woman in the house who will do all our pressing for us."

"That's good to know," Miss Briggs said. "Is it the same one who does the washing?"

Miss Smith nodded.

"I thought you would have known about her if you have been here before."

"I didn't mention her because I thought she might have left," Miss Briggs said quickly.

But she looked so guilty that both Miss Smith and Tempera knew she had deliberately kept the information to herself.

"I gave her a blouse of Her Ladyship's to do," Miss Smith said, "and it was back in an hour looking absolutely perfect!"

"I see I must renew my acquaintance with her," Miss Briggs said in such an artificial tone that it was obvious she had done that already.

Tempera, however, was quite certain that she and her Stepmother could not afford to spend money on anything she could do herself.

Some of the fifteen pounds which Lady Rothley had won last night could well be expended on materials with which she could make her Stepmother new nightgowns and on ribbons and lace to further refurbish the older gowns she had worn before.

Tempera was sure that such things would be far cheaper in France than in England and she thought that as soon as she had the opportunity she would ask Colonel Anstruther if there was any chance of her going into Beaulieu or, better still, Nice.

She had learnt from the other maids that a landau often took the staff shopping.

By the time she had finished washing her Stepmother's underclothes and put them in a spare bathroom to dry, the last vestige of the sun was sinking and the lights on the mountains were very beautiful.

Tempera remembered how lovely the moonlight had been on the sea last night when she had looked out the window.

She decided that tonight she would take the opportunity when the Château was empty to walk along the edge of the cliff and look out to sea with the whole vista of the coast beneath her.

She had seen from the windows that there was a

path and that the edge of the cliff was protected by a low brick wall which was covered with bougainvillaea.

It would be impossible for her to go that way in the daytime because the path could be seen from the terrace, but now there was nobody about except the servants and she had learnt that Colonel Anstruther always retired to bed early.

It was a very warm night and Tempera took off the black gown she had worn during the day and which she thought constituted a uniform suitable to her position.

Instead she put on a pale mauve muslin which she had made herself after her father's death.

It was very plain, but it had a frill of white chiffon round the neck and it made her look very young.

Then in case it grew cold she took over her arm a light woollen shawl, slipped out of the house unobserved, and started to walk along the cliff's edge.

As she did so the last remaining glow of the sun faded and now there was that translucent moment between dusk and night.

The first evening star glittered overhead and there was a strange luminosity over the world, as if the night cast a magic spell over sleeping mortals.

The fragrance of flowers was very strong and every step she took made Tempera feel as if she walked into a strange enchantment she had never known before.

Now the path grew narrower and passed between bushes covered with scented blossoms, and steps climbed upwards through what was a tunnel of greenery.

Finally Tempera found herself on a platform of marble with four exquisite Grecian pillars supporting a flat roof.

There was a wrought-iron balustrade to prevent one from falling over the precipice which was a sheer drop onto bare rocks.

There was a seat on which one could sit looking not only towards the sea but also right towards the high cliffs above the port of Villefranche and left towards the heights of Eze.

It was all very lovely and Tempera gave a little sigh of utter contentment as she sat down.

She felt omnipotent, as the gods and goddesses must have felt as they contemplated the human world below Mt. Olympus.

She looked up at the stars and said a little prayer of thankfulness that she had been brought quite unexpectedly to this enchanted place.

She knew that this was a moment when she must look, listen, and feel, as her father had taught her to do.

This was the sort of scene the great Masters had tried to capture, and yet however great their genius even they could not accurately portray the utter perfection of nature.

It made Tempera feel as she had when she looked at the *Madonna in the Church,* as if the beauty of it pierced into the very depths of her soul and evoked a response that was different from anything she had ever felt before.

How long she sat there in a reverie that was half-prayer, half-ecstasy, she had no idea.

The last vestige of daylight was swept away by the sable darkness of the night, and the moon, a silver crescent against the sky, shone out to add its mystical light to the glory of the stars.

They seemed to dazzle Tempera's eyes, and when suddenly she heard a step and there was a dark shadow between her and the sky she looked up in a bemused manner, not certain if it was real or a part of her imagination.

"I thought I would find you here," said a voice she recognised. "I could not believe that anyone who paints could resist this view."

Tempera did not answer.

She felt for a moment as if it was right for the Duke to be there, and yet somewhere too far away in the distance for her to hear it clearly a voice told her that she should rise and leave.

He sat down beside her and she turned her face to look at him, then because she was shy looked away again.

"And who do you think could paint such beauty?" he asked gently.

Because he compelled her to speak, Tempera answered him honestly:

"I think only Turner could do it justice."

"You are thinking of *Moonlight at Greenwich*."

"Yes, but this is far more lovely."

"I agree with you, and perhaps Turner was better at sunrises."

"*Sunrise with the Sea-Monsters*," Tempera murmured.

Suddenly a thought struck her.

"If everybody has . . . returned . . . Her—Her Ladyship will . . . want me."

She would have risen but the Duke put out his hand and laid it on her arm.

"Nobody has returned except myself," he answered. "I dislike gambling and prefer to look at the moonlight."

The touch of his hand gave Tempera a very strange feeling.

It was almost as if it was part of what she had been feeling in her soul, something that throbbed in her heart. It was not only a feeling, it was thought and yet much more than thought.

Because her own thoughts frightened her she said after a moment:

"I have to . . . thank Your Grace for the . . . canvasses."

"Have you finished your picture?"

"Yes."

"I half-hoped to find it waiting for me."

Tempera did not answer and after a moment the Duke said:

"You intend to let me see it? It was the condition I imposed, if you remember."

He took his hand from her arm as he spoke and Tempera had an absurd feeling that she wanted to ask him to let it remain there.

Then she said after a moment:

"I p-put the picture on your desk this afternoon, but I . . . took it away again."

"Why?"

"I thought the pictures in your room were . . . looking at it scornfully."

"I do not believe there was ever a great Master who scorned a willing and dedicated pupil."

"I cannot quote you an instance," Tempera replied, "but I am certain they were very scornful of those who were . . . presumptuous."

"I am sure that is something you would never be."

Once again Tempera thought that this was a very strange conversation and one she should not be having with the Duke.

"I want to see your picture now that you have finished it," he said, "and I shall feel that you have broken your word if you do not give it to me tomorrow."

"How can it possibly interest you?" Tempera asked almost passionately. "You possess pictures which are so wonderful, so perfect, that all I would ask of life would be to look at them and understand what they are trying to . . . say."

The words seemed to be forced from her, and even as she heard her own voice dying away in the stillness she thought again how reprehensible all this was.

"About which picture in particular do you feel like that?" the Duke asked.

Tempera paused.

She had meant to leave to her Stepmother the one which moved her most of all, and she felt it would be betraying her trust if she told the truth.

"Tell me," the Duke asked. "I want to know."

There was a note of command in his voice. It seemed to Tempera to vibrate through her and at the same time compel her to tell him what he wanted to know.

It was something he had done ever since they had met, she thought, compelling her to behave in a way she did not wish; compelling her to talk to him; compelling her to reveal her secret thoughts that were hers and hers alone.

Almost as if he felt she resented his authority, he said in a very different voice:

"I am waiting. Please tell me."

As if it was impossible to resist him, Tempera answered:

"The *Madonna in the Church*."

Without looking at him she knew he smiled.

"I might have guessed that was the one," he said. "It is my favourite and I bought it myself. It was not in my father's collection."

"There is something about ... it which is ... different," Tempera murmured.

"I know," the Duke agreed. "It is nothing that can be expressed in words, but it is there, and I know that we both feel the same about it."

"Perhaps Artists like van Eyck painted what they saw not with their eyes but ... with their ... souls."

Tempera did not know why she went on trying to express what the Duke had already said was inexpressible.

She turned her head after she had spoken and found he was nearer to her than she had expected, and in the moonlight it was easy to see his face.

His eyes were on hers and she had a feeling that he looked deep into her heart and they spoke to each other with their souls.

For a long, long moment she was very still.

Then with what was a physical effort she rose to her feet, saying almost incoherently:

"I ... must go ... Your Grace. Thank you for your kindness ... but it is getting late."

"Not too late for there to be a likelihood of any-one returning from the Paradise of gamblers."

The scathing note in the Duke's voice was un-mistakable, and Tempera realised with a sense of guilt that, knowing he hated gambling, she should have told her Stepmother to say it bored her too.

Belle-mère should have returned with him—that was obvious.

'It is the second time she has let the Duke slip away on his own while she stayed on at the Casino,' Tempera thought.

"What are you thinking about?" the Duke asked.

He had not risen when Tempera had, but now slowly he did so and she felt as if he towered over her.

"I am ... finding it difficult to ... express my thoughts, Your Grace."

"There is no need. Nor should you thank me. The moonlight and the sea are free for those who can in-terpret them."

She felt as her whole being responded to the note in his voice, and there was something else, the close-ness of him, the sudden realisation that he was a man and she was a woman and they were alone together.

She looked up into his face, her eyes very wide and dark in the moonlight.

Then because she longed to stay and because she knew that he wanted her to do so, she turned and hur-ried away.

She walked quickly until she descended the steps and was moving through the green tunnel which the moonlight intersected with silver beams.

Then suddenly she began to run wildly in a panic-stricken manner towards the safety of the lighted Château.

Chapter Four

It was only when Tempera had put her Stepmother to bed and was alone in the darkness of her own room that she could think clearly of what she had said to the Duke as they sat in the moonlight.

It was then, she told herself, that once again she had behaved in an extremely reprehensible manner, and most of all her behaviour with regard to the picture was inexcusable.

It was all so simple.

Out of his charity he had given her some canvasses and he had asked in return that he should see the picture she had painted of his flowers.

Why in those circumstances should she behave like a self-conscious, hysterical school-girl?

All she had to do was to leave the picture on his desk as she had intended, and if he wished to keep it, there was no reason why she should argue.

He had recompensed her most generously, and to keep repeating that her work was not good enough and all the other foolish things she had said would, she knew, have aroused her father's contempt.

He had disliked Artists who disparaged their own work in the hope that they would be contradicted.

"There is nothing more infuriating," he had said often enough, "than those who are too humble. I prefer those who blow their own trumpet loudly."

Tempera had laughed.

"I do not believe you, Papa! You would slap down anybody who was boastful about a painting you did not consider good enough."

"An Artist should have self-confidence in his Art," her father had replied evasively.

But she had known what he meant and now it seemed to her she was being excessively, obsequiously humble, instead of accepting her work at its face value, as apparently the Duke was prepared to do.

Where she was at fault was that instead of thinking of his interest as a kind gesture from a nobleman to a servant, she had talked to him almost as if she were his equal.

"Everything had gone wrong since the moment he first found me painting in the garden," she told herself miserably.

And yet she was honest enough to admit that it had been a delight that she had never anticipated to sit with him looking at that exquisite and perfect view of sea and sky and know that he understood what she was feeling.

She wondered how many other men at this moment in the South of France, intent on gambling at Monte Carlo, would have had the least comprehension of what she and the Duke had discussed—certainly none of the men her Stepmother knew.

Then she told herself that this was a dangerous path to follow.

The Duke must not become interested in her, even in a very perfunctory way.

He must be made to concentrate his attention on her Stepmother.

'There is no danger of my damaging *Belle-mère*'s chances where the Duke is concerned,' Tempera thought. 'We are not in the same category. At the same time, any diversion from the main objective is dangerous.'

She turned restlessly over and over on her pillow,

trying to think how she could in some way extract herself from this embarrassing situation.

It was foolish to pretend that she had not aroused the Duke's interest; for it was indeed unusual to find a servant painting as well as she could.

At the same time, when they were together it was impossible not to realise that where painting was concerned they could talk on a different level from anything her Stepmother could attempt.

"I must not see him again," Tempera told herself, and knew that something within her rebelled at the thought.

At the same time, she had to be practical: the first thing was to rid herself of her obligation over the picture—and then to hope that once having received it the Duke would shut it away in a drawer and forget about it.

She decided that the sooner it was in his possession, the better. Like all men, he would be irritated at not obtaining what he desired.

Too late now, she wished she had left it on his desk when she had first put it there.

Tempera found it impossible to sleep and as the stars began to fade she decided what she would do.

She would slip downstairs before the household was aroused, put the picture in the Duke's room, then determinedly keep out of his way so that there would be no question of his demanding to see any other picture she might paint.

She was well aware that she would have to do this very early; otherwise, during the rest of the day there would be people moving about and she might be seen.

She had no wish to explain even to her Stepmother what had occurred, and the idea of encountering Lord Eustace again made her shudder.

She thought that if she went downstairs as soon as it was dawn she would be safe enough.

She had learnt that the Duke, always considerate of his guests' comfort, had given orders that the Sit-

ting-Rooms which were below the main bed-rooms
were not to be cleaned too early in the morning in case
the noise should disturb those sleeping above.

There was just the faintest glow in the sky, enough
to cast a light through the long windows in the hall, as
Tempera slipped along the passage and reached the
top of the stairs.

She thought that with her thin white wrap over her
nightgown she must look almost like a ghost in the
shadowy light and thought with a smile of amusement
that if any of the housemaids saw her they might
scream.

Because her bed-room faced the back of the
Château she usually heard the awakening staff but
there was still no sound of them and in the huge cool
hall there was only an utter quiet and the fragrance
of lilies.

In her heel-less slippers she crossed the marble
floor. She could have entered the Duke's private room
through a door in the hall, but she chose to go through
the Sitting-Room.

Here the curtains were drawn, but there was
enough glow from the sky percolating through the sides
of them for her to be able to see her way.

The Rubens and the Ricci were dark against the
white of the walls, very different from the flash of
brilliant colour they were in the daytime.

Tempera walked round the deep, soft sofas and
comfortable arm-chairs towards the door which led into the Duke's room.

She held her picture in both hands and thought
that she would prop it up against the big silver ink-pot
on the Duke's desk. She wondered how soon it would be
before he turned it over and saw the inscription on the
back.

Then as she reached the open door and was just
about to step inside she realised that there was someone
there already.

She stopped still and her heart gave a strange

leap, although whether it was from fear or excitement she did not know.

Then she realised that one of the curtains was pulled back and she could see quite clearly that the man standing with his back to her was not the Duke.

In a flash she recognised the carriage of the head—it was Lord Eustace.

For a moment it was hard to breathe and impossible even to move. Then silently on tip-toe Tempera turned and running from the Sitting-Room sped through the hall and up the stairs.

Only when she reached the sanctuary of her own room did she realise that her breath was coming quickly and her heart was throbbing.

Lord Eustace! She might have encountered him dressed as she was in her thin wrap and nightgown!

She was only too well aware of what his reaction would have been, and she would have had no-one to blame but herself.

She supposed that like her he could not sleep.

She knew that he had gone to his own room when her Stepmother had returned, because she had heard the party saying good-night to one another as they went up the stairs.

"Good-night, Lady Holcombe," Lady Rothley had said, raising her voice a little so that if Tempera was asleep she would wake up.

"Good-night, Lady Rothley. I am sure you enjoyed yourself tonight."

There was just a little note of spite in Lady Holcombe's voice and she accentuated the word "enjoyed."

"Very much," Lady Rothley answered. "Good-night, Lady Barnard."

"Good-night, my dear, you were very much admired. Everybody in the Casino who did not know you already was asking who you were."

"Thank you," Lady Rothley replied. "You are very kind."

"That is what we always try to be," Lady Barnard answered, and Tempera heard her going down the passage towards her own bed-room.

Then as Lady Rothley had come into the room to fling her wrap down on the bed and cross to the mirror to look at her reflection, Tempera had heard the Duke's voice and could not help standing listening to it.

"Good-night, George," he said, speaking to Lord Holcombe. "Good-night, Eustace."

"Good-night, Velde," Lord Eustace answered.

"I hope you are quite comfortable in the Tower," the Duke said. "It is where I always used to sleep and it has a better view than any other room in the Château."

"Your hospitality is always superlative, Velde," Lord Eustace replied. "My only complaint is that, while I feel 'Monarch of all I survey,' I am at times a little lonely."

The Duke laughed.

"What you are suggesting is the only comfort I do not feel qualified to supply!"

Both men laughed and moved away, and while she could hear their voices in the distance Tempera could not discern what they said.

She wondered now if it was because he felt lonely that Lord Eustace had been unable to sleep.

Whatever the reason, he had come downstairs unaccountably early, and it was only by the greatest good fortune that he had not realised she was there.

"He is yet another man I must avoid," she told herself.

Then getting into bed she continued to lie sleepless until it was time to get up.

* * *

All morning Tempera tried to plan when she would have an opportunity to leave the picture on the Duke's desk.

She had an uncomfortable feeling that if Colonel Anstruther saw it he would ask questions as to why it was there, and she felt a sudden shrinking within herself against anyone else knowing that she painted or that she had promised her picture to the Duke.

Then somehow she had an inner conviction that he would know that that was what she felt, and he would not talk of her talent to his Comptroller and certainly not to his other guests.

She had no good reason for thinking this. Yet there was a certainty within herself that the Duke would understand her feelings and respect them.

There were quite a lot of things to do in the morning for her Stepmother.

The hem of one of her gowns had come undone, and there was a spot on the front of one of the most expensive and most elaborate of Lucille's models.

It required removing very delicately so as not to affect the colour of the material, and it took Tempera a considerable time, in fact longer than to mend the hem.

This morning Lady Rothley was drowsy and inclined to be petulant.

She was always rather an indolent person, taking no exercise except on the Ball-Room floor or moving serenely over a green lawn, and she was not used to the very late hours that were customary in the South of France.

"I suppose I could not stay in bed today," she suggested after she had eaten her breakfast.

Tempera looked at her in horror.

"How can you suggest such a thing, *Belle-mère?* You know every hour, every minute, is precious. Besides, I have learnt there is a luncheon-party here today."

Lady Rothley gave a little scream.

"But of course there is! And the Count is coming! He told me so last night. This is exciting! I feel better already. I will have my bath, Tempera, then you shall do my hair and make me look really beautiful."

"Who is this Count?" Tempera asked. "We have

talked about him often enough, but I have never asked
you his name."

"He has a terrible name! I have the greatest difficulty in pronouncing it," Lady Rothley answered. "It
is Caravargio—that is it! Count Vincenzo Caravargio
—Heavens, what a mouthful!"

"Are you sure?" Tempera questioned.

"Of course I am sure," Lady Rothley replied.

"But Vincenzo Caravargio was a friend of Papa's."

"Yes, I know. He told me so."

"Then listen, *Belle-mère,* I have met him, so you
must be very careful what you say."

"You could not have made much of an impression. He has never spoken about you, although he has
talked of your father. Apparently they had the same
interests."

"But of course they did," Tempera said almost
impatiently. "Do you not know, *Belle-mère,* that
Count Vincenzo Caravargio has one of the most famous collections of sculpture in the whole of Italy?
The Villa Caravargio outside Rome is famous, almost
as well known as the Villa Borghese, and Papa often
spoke of it."

"I am not interested in his possessions, and if
you try to describe a lot of statues to me I shall
scream!" Lady Rothley said. "I am interested in the
Count. If you only knew the delightful things that he
says in that deep Latin voice of his."

"*Belle-mère,* listen to me," Tempera begged. "I
have heard Papa talk of the Count ever since I was a
little girl. I know that he was married when he was
very young and was extremely unhappy in consequence. He has been a widower for ten, perhaps fifteen years, and I am sure he has no intention of
marrying again."

"He certain does not speak of marriage, but of
love!" Lady Rothley said.

"*Belle-mère,* how can you listen? You know as

well as I do that there are hundreds of men who want to make love to you because you are so beautiful. But we are interested in finding you a husband."

"I know," Lady Rothley agreed. "You are quite right, Tempera, but husbands never seem to say the same fascinating things that the Count says so eloquently."

Tempera almost wrung her hands in despair.

"What am I to say to you?" she asked. "You know why we are here. You know the Duke is interested in you, otherwise he would not have invited you. But now you are spending your time not with him but with this Italian, whose intentions I am quite certain do not include a wedding-ring."

Lady Rothley turned from the contemplation of her face in the mirror to look at her Stepdaughter.

"You are so sweet and so sensible, Tempera," she said, "but you are trying to spoil my fun and I am enjoying myself so much."

She spoke like a child who was told she could not have another iced cake. But Tempera did not smile; instead, she said almost despairingly:

"I want you to be happy, *Belle-mère,* I want you to have all the fun in the world, but you know we cannot afford it. Have you forgotten that when we get home there will be innumerable bills waiting for us: the rates, Agnes's wages, the ground rent, oh—a thousand other things!"

Lady Rothley rose from the dressing-table to walk to the window.

She looked out over the sea but she was not admiring the view.

"Shall I be truthful, Tempera," she asked, "and tell you that I am attracted by the Count? Perhaps more than I have ever before been attracted by a man."

"But he is an Italian . . . a Catholic. He will not marry you," Tempera replied, "although he may ask you to be his mistress."

"I think he may do so," Lady Rothley said in a low voice, "and I am wondering what my answer will be."

"Belle-mère!"

Tempera was shocked. There was no doubt about that, and the note in her voice made her Stepmother turn to see the expression on her face.

She moved towards her and put her arms round her.

"Do not look like that, dearest," she begged. "It is wrong of me—I know it is wrong—but I cannot help myself."

She held Tempera close to her for a moment, then she walked across the room to fling herself down on the bed.

"I know now," she said, almost as if she were talking to herself, "that all my life I have been what is called a cold woman. I thought I was in love with the man to whom I was engaged, but while I was very fond of Harry and wept bitterly when he was killed, it never meant very much to me when he kissed me."

She paused and did not look at Tempera as she went on:

"When I met your father and he fell in love with me I admired him and thought him charming, and it was very exciting to be Lady Rothley."

Tempera wanted to beg her not to go on, but somehow the words would not come to her lips.

"I was devoted to Francis," her Stepmother continued in a low voice. "I felt safe with him, and I had never known before what it was to be important and to meet exciting people."

"Please . . . *Belle-mère,*" Tempera said almost beneath her breath.

But she realised that her Stepmother was not really talking to her but sorting things out in her own mind.

"When he made love to me I wanted to please him and I thought that all a woman had to do in love-making was to be acquiescent. I did not know—I had no idea that I could feel as I feel now."

Tempera gave a deep sigh and sat down on the stool in front of the dressing-table.

"When the Count talks to me," Lady Rothley murmured, "I feel little ripples of excitement going down my spine and when he kisses my hand I want him to kiss my lips and I want . . ."

She stopped.

"You are too young, Tempera, for me to be talking to you like this. But sometimes I feel as if you were older than I and that I, in reality, am only a very young girl who has never before woken up to find she is a—woman."

Quite unexpectedly Lady Rothley's voice broke on the last word, and the tears were running from her blue eyes down her pink-and-white cheeks.

"Oh, Tempera," she exclaimed in a broken voice, "what am I to do?"

It was impossible for Tempera to resist the appeal for help and she rose from the stool to go to the bed and put her arms round her Stepmother.

"It is all right, dearest, do not cry," she begged. "We will find a way out of this somehow."

"How? How?" Lady Rothley sobbed. "You are quite right, Tempera, I am sure he will not marry me . . . but I love him! That is the truth. I love him madly, wildly, crazily, so that it is impossible to think straight!"

Could anything be more disastrous, Tempera thought, than that this should happen at this moment?

But she could not bear to see her Stepmother in tears, realising how seldom she cried.

She wiped the tears from her cheeks, talking to her almost as if she were a small child.

"You must not cry, you will make yourself look plain! The Count and the Duke will be there at luncheon, both admiring you, both thinking you are the most beautiful woman they have ever seen! You must not disappoint them."

Lady Rothley sat up and blew her nose almost defiantly.

"Supposing neither of them offers me ... anything?" she asked despondently.

"I think we can be sure of what the Count will offer you," Tempera said with a touch of irony in her voice. "I know from what I have heard about him that he is an inveterate flirt, and there is nothing to stop you once you are a Duchess from going on flirting with him."

"How could I ... marry anybody else when I ... love him?" Lady Rothley asked.

Her voice was so unhappy that Tempera thought she was in fact right when she said she felt like a young girl.

She might pretend to be sophisticated, she might wish to move in a Society where married women took lovers and artistocratic marriages were arranged almost the way they were in France; but now that she was in love, she was just as moon-struck as any peasant-girl might be.

All the time Tempera was dressing her, Lady Rothley talked of the Count, veering between an ecstatic description of his attractions and moments of despondency because she could mean nothing in his life.

It was Tempera who tried to bring the conversation down to the commonplace.

"What you have to decide, *Belle-mère,* is what you will say if the Count asks you to be his mistress."

Lady Rothley made a little choked sound, but she did not speak and Tempera went on:

"You know as well as I do that if you agree, your position in Society will be ruined forever. You cannot go away with the Count, then come back to England as if nothing had happened."

She paused before she continued:

"From all you have told me, it is obvious that love-affairs amongst the aristocracy are always extremely discreet. The two people concerned meet at the big house-parties they attend, and they are invited together; but everybody pretends it is just by chance!"

"That is true," Lady Rothley murmured.

"When the liaison is over," Tempera went on, "I gather that they return to their respective husbands and wives as if nothing had happened."

As Lady Rothley did not speak Tempera said positively:

"But you have no husband, *Belle-mère*, no-one to protect you from the scandal which you will arouse if you live with a man as important and well-known as the Count."

"He would not leave me ... penniless," Lady Rothley said faintly.

"He might leave you with money, but nothing else," Tempera retorted. "What good would money be if you were not asked to the Balls, Receptions, and parties you enjoy so much? You know as well as I do that the doors of houses like the Duke's would be closed to you."

"What you are telling me is true, and you are quite right," Lady Rothley said pathetically, "but I love him, Tempera, I love him!"

Tempera thought the tears were likely to begin again and so she soothed her Stepmother, arranged her hair in a new and becoming fashion, and dressed her in one of her prettiest gowns.

"Forget the future and enjoy the present," she admonished her. "You were a success last night! Go downstairs and be a success today, darling *Belle-mère!* As Papa often said when he was irritated: 'Tomorrow will come to reckoning—but be damned to it!' "

"Tempera!"

Lady Rothley looked quite shocked at the swear-word, and then she laughed.

"Oh, Tempera, I love you! Could any woman ever have a kinder and more adorable Stepdaughter?"

With the quick change of mood her face lit up and her eyes were smiling.

"The sun is shining," she said. "We are staying

with a Duke and there is a Count waiting to make love to me. What more could any woman want?"

"Nothing, except to look as beautiful as you," Tempera replied.

"I will go down and dazzle them!" Lady Rothley said. "And it is one satisfaction to know that Rosie Holcombe is longing to scratch my eyes out!"

She went from the room, leaving Tempera laughing, but the smile faded and she sat down on a chair rather helplessly, thinking of the mess they were in.

She tried to remember all her father had told her about the Count in the past.

She had met him twice or perhaps three times, but he had not paid any attention to her as she had been at that time a school-girl.

Yet she had the feeling that his dark eyes missed nothing and that he had a retentive memory.

'Whatever happens, he must not catch a glimpse of me,' she thought.

It suddenly came to her how much it would damage her Stepmother if it was learnt that she was employing her own Stepdaughter as a lady's-maid.

It was the kind of tit-bit of gossip which would spread like wild-fire amongst the people who had nothing better to do than to chitter-chatter about one another.

It would doubtless be magnified and exaggerated into a kind of fairy-story about the wicked Stepmother who beat and oppressed the pretty heroine.

"I shall have to keep out of sight," Tempera told herself, "not only of the Count but also of the Duke, and of course Lord Eustace!"

The last thought was reinforced by what she heard when she joined the two other lady's-maids at luncheon.

Tempera learnt that Lady Holcombe had lost quite a considerable sum at Baccarat the previous night, and she and her husband had had some very unpleasant words about it.

Sir William Barnard, on the other hand, because

he was so rich, had won a small fortune; but there had been trouble in the Casino because a woman had accused him of collecting her winnings along with his own.

How the maids learnt of these things Tempera had no idea, but they always had something to relate to each other and she in fact was the only person who did not contribute anything to the conversation.

"I can tell you one thing," Miss Briggs said as they were drinking the large cups of tea which accompanied every meal.

"What's that?" Miss Smith enquired.

"His Lordship's up to his tricks again."

"Do you mean Lord Eustace?"

"Who else?" Miss Briggs demanded with a note of contempt in her voice.

"What's he done now?" Miss Smith asked.

"As I was going along to Her Ladyship's room this morning I heard what sounded like screams and a lot of giggling coming from the direction of the Tower," Miss Briggs replied.

"You did?" Miss Smith ejaculated, her eyes alert with interest.

"I dropped something by accident," Miss Briggs, said, "and while I was picking it up the door of His Lordship's room opened and out came Madeleine."

"Which one's that?" Miss Smith asked.

"The big, bosomy girl who I always think is cheeky when I can understand what she's saying," Miss Briggs replied.

"Oh, I know her," Miss Smith said. "I wouldn't trust her far, and that's a fact."

"And you would be quite right," Miss Briggs agreed. "Her hair was untidy, her apron crumped, and as she shut the door behind her I had a glimpse of His Lordship in his shirt-sleeves."

"Well, I never!" Miss Smith exclaimed. "You'd think he'd leave the chamber-maids alone."

"Not him," Miss Briggs said with satisfaction. "He's always the same. I remember two years ago when we were staying in the North with the Duke of Hull . . ."

She started off on a long story of Lord Eustace's predilection for a pretty maid-servant, but Tempera was not listening.

She was reliving the lucky escape she had had this morning and reflecting upon how, after the way he had looked at her when they first met, she knew she must keep out of his way.

He was the sort of gentleman who, she had heard, seduced lonely young Governesses who were then dismissed without a reference.

'He is despicable!' she thought. 'I cannot believe that the Duke is aware of his behaviour—otherwise he would not have him to stay.'

The thought struck her almost like a dagger that perhaps the Duke also found servants fair game. Then she was ashamed that the thought had even crossed her mind.

How could any man who had understood what she was trying to say about looking and listening to the beauty of the night not be honourable and straightforward in his behaviour?

However Lord Eustace might behave, she would stake her soul on the Duke's complete and absolute integrity.

And yet she had to avoid him also.

It was a depressing thought, but she told herself that she must do nothing which might prevent him from admiring her Stepmother.

It was absurd to think that she might interest him as a woman; but she might as an Artist, which was a different thing, though still a diversion.

She was quite certain that if the Duke should propose marriage to *Belle-mère*, there would be no question after that of her philandering with the Count.

No woman who liked Society would refuse to be a Duchess, and, as Tempera well knew, her Stepmother loved the Social World and longed to be a shining star in its glittering firmament.

She only hoped that Lady Rothley would not

show too obviously her preference for the alluring Count.

He had seemed very old to Tempera when she was a child because he was nearing her father's age; but when she thought about him she could remember dark, flashing eyes in a lean face with aristocratic features which declared him obviously a patrician.

She could remember his voice, too, deep and somehow resonant, and she thought as she looked back that he often seemed to be laughing.

'It is just what *Belle-mère* would enjoy,' she thought, 'the frothy gaiety of champagne, which the Count can offer her, when what she will have to prefer is the solid fare of an English meal.'

She laughed a little at the metaphor, then told herself it was really very serious.

The only eventuality she had not foreseen on this adventure they had undertaken together was that *Belle-mère*, of all people, would fall in love for the first time in her life.

Because that, Tempera knew, was what had happened.

She was in love and the only thing that could save her from taking a disastrous step in the wrong direction would be her inherent sense of snobbery.

It was all so perplexing that when Tempera reached her bed-room she stood for a long time irresolute just inside the door, so bemused by her thoughts that she was not even certain where she was.

Then suddenly she told herself that if she intended to put the picture downstairs on the Duke's desk this was the moment.

The house-party was having luncheon on the terrace.

They had been eating for less than an hour and Tempera knew that any meal would take twice, if not three times, as long as that.

It was delightful on the terrace with the bougainvillaea climbing up the walls and over the railings which bordered the deep precipice on the side of which the Château was built.

The terrace was paved and there were awnings to protect those who sat or ate there from the sun. It must be, Tempera thought, rather like being in an eagle's-nest, high above the world, but secure and safe.

The men-servants were all engaged in waiting at the luncheon and by now the housemaids would have tidied the Sitting-Room and there would be nobody there.

This was the chance, Tempera guessed, for which she had been waiting.

Picking up her picture, she walked very carefully down the stairs, thinking that if she should meet anybody her excuse about the loss of a handkerchief would serve as well as any other.

The Sitting-Room was, however, empty, and there was only the sound of voices laughing and talking in the distance.

Tempera took a fleeting glance at the pictures as she passed them, almost as if she greeted them as old friends.

Then she entered the Duke's room and found to her relief that this time there was no-one there.

She put her picture down on the desk and felt as she did so that she had taken an irrevocable step towards behaving from now on in a very different manner.

She would not make the same mistakes again, and even if it meant that she must stay indoors at night she would not risk meeting the Duke in the moonlight.

That constituted a danger to her plans not only for her Stepmother but also for herself.

She was not prepared to explain why, but in her heart she knew the reason and would not face it.

On the Duke's desk was a huge blotter with silver edges with his monogram also in silver emblazoned on the leather cover.

The ink-pot was very beautiful and Tempera was certain that it was made in the time of Charles II and extremely rare.

She could not help looking at it for a moment before she propped her picture against it. Then, having done so, almost as if it drew her irresistibly she raised her eyes to Leonardo da Vinci's angel.

Whoever had painted the reproduction had done it very skilfully, and Tempera was certain that the Artist had copied it from the original picture in the Louvre and not from the one in the National Gallery.

"Am I really like that?" she asked herself.

It was difficult to be sure.

The angel's sweet, sensitive face was so engraved on her mind that it was as familiar as the reflection she saw in her own mirror.

And what did the Duke think?

Tempera told herself that if in fact he had thought she resembled the angel whom he faced every time he wrote a letter, he would have mentioned it to her.

They had been so close last night that she had almost known what he was thinking and that he had been aware of what she was trying to express.

It would have been simple for him to say when they had spoken of the pictures in his room that her face in some small way reminded him of the one which Leonardo da Vinci had painted 421 years ago.

'Perhaps he will think of it later,' Tempera thought, then shied away from the implication.

She moved towards the door and as she did so she could not help lingering for one moment to take another look at the *Madonna in the Church*.

'It stands out,' she thought, 'like a glittering diamond even among the other jewels this room contains.'

Her eyes lingered on the red of the Madonna's robe, the crown on her head, the sunlight coming through the Gothic windows of the Church. Then suddenly Tempera was very still.

She stared at the picture, drew nearer, and stared again.

She shut her eyes and blinked, then put her face to the left in order to behold it from another angle.

There was something strange, something she had not noticed before—or had she forgotten?

She could not explain to herself what had happened, but the picture looked different.

She told herself she was imagining things. It must be exactly the same as when she first saw it, when it had given her an irresistible excitement because it was the most beautiful thing she had ever seen.

But now it did not arouse the same feeling in her as it had done before. It did not speak to her, its spirituality did not reach out to touch some chord within herself.

What was wrong? What was the difference?

Tempera put out her hands and lifting the picture from its hook took it to the window.

She stared at it for some moments, then turned it over and looked at the back.

As she did so, she knew, without obvious proof but with a conviction that was unshakeable, that the picture was a fake!

* * *

Tempera walked through the arched entrance gate and stepping off the roadway took a winding path which was little more than a sheep-track down into the valley.

She walked through an olive grove until she was out of sight of the Château, then she sat down on the grass beside a small ravine.

At any other time she would have been thrilled by the blue-green of borage and hyacinth and the yellow and red of the jonquils and wild anemones.

But as she now sat with her back against the twisting trunk of an ancient olive tree she was concerned only with the problem that seemed to fill her mind with darkness.

It was as if suddenly, as she walked along in the sunshine, a vast chasm had opened at her feet and she could not pass over it or get round it.

There was no doubt in her mind what had happened.

It was as clear as if someone had told her with an undeniable authority that a fake *Madonna in the Church* had been substituted for the original.

There was also no doubt as to who had done it.

Why else had Lord Eustace been up so early in the morning? And why had he been in the Duke's special Sanctum?

And, as Tempera realised now, he had actually been standing in front of the picture.

He might, she thought, have just at that moment substituted the fake for the real and stood back to see the effect.

If she had come into the Sitting-Room a few minutes later she would doubtless have missed him.

Even though she would still have recognised the picture as being false, she would have had no idea who was the thief.

There was no doubt now, but the difficulty was what should she do about it.

She was well aware that the fake was an extremely good one, but there were, as she knew, Artists in Europe who could copy a picture so skilfully that they could deceive even the experts.

She thought that if she had not examined the *Madonna in the Church* so closely when she first saw it, she might quite easily have been deceived by the copy which now hung in its frame.

But there was something about the original which had aroused an unmistakable response in her.

That was how, as her father had said so often, one listened to what a picture had to say. It was hard to describe, but to her it was an irrefutable method of knowing the real from the false.

"Papa would never for a moment have been deceived by that fake," Tempera told herself. "But I might have been, if it had been of any other picture."

That particular Masterpiece meant something very special to her, just as it meant something to the Duke.

At the thought of him Tempera clasped her hands together and wondered frantically what she should do.

The obvious course, had she been an ordinary guest, would have been to tell him exactly what had occurred so that the thief could be apprehended.

But if she did that, it was inevitable that in the sensation which would ensue, her real identity would be brought to light.

Even if the police were not brought in, which Tempera imagined would be unavoidable where such a valuable possession was concerned, the Duke and his Comptroller would make searching enquiries amongst the servants and everybody would be suspect until they were proved innocent.

In those circumstances suspicions would be bound to fall on her.

After all, she had shown that she could paint, and it could easily be observed that she was not the ordinary lady's-maid she pretended to be!

While Tempera was certain that her name would be cleared eventually, it would be impossible to conceal that she was her father's daughter.

What was more, long before any special enquiry could take place, there was every chance of the Count recognising her, as he was staying in the house.

Tempera's vivid imagination made her see all too clearly the confusion that would ensue if she told the Duke what had happened. The revelations would be not only embarrassing but also devastating as far as her Stepmother was concerned.

She put her hands up to her eyes and tried to think clearly.

The alternative was to do nothing, and hope that they would have left the Château before the Duke discovered what had happened to his picture.

But she had an uncomfortable feeling that long before they had the chance to leave, the Count, when he inspected the Duke's collection, as he was bound to do, would realise, as she had, that something was wrong.

Whichever way it happened she was in a trap, and as far as she could see there was no escape.

"Oh, Papa," Tempera prayed, and it was a cry from her very heart, "wherever you are, help me! I need your help desperately!"

Chapter Five

The more Tempera considered what she should do, the more confused she became.

She felt as if everything had fallen into small pieces round her and she could not put them together again.

There was danger in every course she might take, and even more in doing nothing.

If only the Count were not staying at the Château, then perhaps the deception might not be noticed for a long time.

Many people saw what they expected to see, and the Duke would be so familiar with his picture that even he might merely feel happy to know it was there and would not examine it closely.

But she was quite certain that sooner or later during his visit to the Château the Count would look at every picture on the walls and discuss them with the Duke.

It was the sort of thing that connoisseurs like her father always did.

Even if they had seen a picture hundreds of times before, they would still stand in front of it again, look and appraise it and, as her father had said so often, listen to what it had to say.

"I have to do something," Tempera told herself.

The question was—what?

She sat in the shade of the olive tree, staring with unseeing eyes across the verdant valley, aware of nothing but her own confusion.

She was oblivious to the loveliness of her surroundings, the bees buzzing amongst the flowers, and the fragrance of wild thyme.

Then with a sense of shock which made her start violently she heard an amused voice say:

"I could show you a better hiding-place than this."

She looked up at the Duke, her eyes wide in her heart-shaped face, and thought he seemed larger and more overpowering than ever.

It was impossible to ignore that her whole being responded to the knowledge that he was there and that she was seeing him again.

"What has happened? Why are you looking so worried?" he enquired.

She looked away from him, surprised that he should have noticed and aware that her heart was pounding in a most unaccountable manner.

He sat down beside her amongst the wild flowers.

"What has upset you?" he asked.

Now there was a beguiling note in his voice that Tempera thought she had not heard before.

"It is . . . nothing," she murmured.

Even as she spoke she knew how annoying it was when people made such a silly answer when there was obviously something very wrong.

"That is not . . . quite true," she added quickly, "but it is . . . something I cannot tell Your Grace."

"Why not?" he enquired. "And why have you come out here to hide yourself?"

She did not answer and he said with a smile:

"If you are trying to hide from me, may I say it is impossible. I lived here for months when I was a boy and I know every nook and cranny where it was hard for first my Nurse and then my tutors to find me."

Tempera gave a little sigh.

She knew she longed to ask him about his childhood, to listen to him talking to her in his deep voice that seemed to compel her attention.

Then, remembering her position and the fact that in no circumstances should she be sitting here beside the Duke, she replied:

"If you have finished luncheon, Your Grace, I must go back to the Château. Her Ladyship . . ."

"You are much too late," the Duke interrupted, "and Her Ladyship has no need of your attentions. She has in fact gone driving with the Count in his motor-car."

"Oh, no!" Tempera exclaimed involuntarily.

It was in fact an involuntary reaction to the knowledge that Lady Rothley was with the Count, but fortunately the Duke misunderstood her anxiety.

"There is no need to worry about Her Ladyship's safety," he said. "I can assure you that the Count is a very experienced driver and his car is one of the safest and most up-to-date models in existence. He has entered it for the *Concours d'Élégance* in Monte Carlo."

It was hopeless, Tempera thought, to try to prevent her Stepmother from doing all the things she should not do.

How could she be so foolish as to go off alone with the Count in his car and inevitably link their names together where the gossips were concerned?

"Do not look so anxious," the Duke pleaded. "I am sure, although I am too polite to ask, that Lady Rothley is older than you and quite capable of taking care of herself."

"Her Ladyship is very . . . impulsive," Tempera said slowly, choosing her words with care, "and she is so kind and . . . gentle that she hates to refuse to do anything that is asked of her."

"I can see that although you are too diplomatic to say so, you do not approve of Count Vincenzo Caravargio," the Duke remarked.

"It is not for me in my position to approve or disapprove, Your Grace," Tempera replied. "But I think that Italians have an eloquence which, while it is

to them no more than a form of good manners, is often
misunderstood by Englishwomen."

"How do you know such things?" the Duke asked.
"I cannot believe that at your age and in the life you
have chosen, Miss Riley, you have had much experience of Italians."

Too late, Tempera realised as she had spoken that
she had fallen into yet another quick-sand.

It had been her intention to make the Duke understand how simple and inexperienced her Stepmother
was, but she thought perhaps she had merely made
things worse rather than better.

The Duke was looking at her profile silhouetted
against the bare rocks of the ravine at their side, and
when neither of them was speaking there was the
sound of water from a small cascade falling into a pool
below.

"I have not been here for many years," the Duke
said conversationally, "and you might find it useful to
know that a little further down there is a cave in the
side of the ravine which none of my tutors ever discovered."

Tempera felt he was teasing her, and she thought
it was something he should not be allowed to do.

"I am . . . not hiding from anybody, Your Grace,"
she said, "and I am sure I should . . . return to the
Château and that . . . you should not be here with me."

"Who is to say what I should or should not do?"
the Duke enquired. "I am my own master."

"Y-yes . . . of course I realise that," Tempera replied quickly, "but if anyone saw us here they would
think it very . . . strange."

"I think it is very unlikely that anyone will see
us," the Duke said, "and that is why you came here in
the first place."

"I certainly did not . . . expect Your Grace to . . .
follow me."

"I am aware of that," he replied, "but surely you
knew I should wish to thank you for the present of

your picture? You did mean it as a present, did you not?"

There was a little pause before Tempera said:

"If . . . Your Grace really wishes to . . . keep it."

"I certainly do wish to, and may I say in words which need no Italian eloquence that I consider you have a very outstanding talent and a feeling for colour which is unusual."

Tempera felt the blush rising in her cheeks.

"Your Grace is . . . very kind."

"I expected to find you painting this afternoon," the Duke said. "Surely the canvasses were what you wanted?"

"Yes . . . of course," Tempera stammered.

"But I know the answer to my own question," the Duke went on. "It lies in the fact that you have a problem which you will not share with me."

Tempera made a little gesture with her hands.

How could she make him understand, she wondered, that even while there was no question of her sharing her troubles with him, he should not be sitting here talking to her, while her Stepmother was philandering with the Count, who would only destroy her socially."

"Many people have brought me their problems at one time or another," the Duke said softly, "and I pride myself that it has been the exception for me not to be able to help them and give them the advice they needed. I would like you to trust me."

"That is impossible! Quite . . . quite . . . impossible!"

Tempera spoke passionately because she found it hard to resist the pleading in his voice. Then she said:

"Your Grace must excuse me. I know you think I am behaving very foolishly, but this is something for which only I can find the answer."

"Are you sure of that?" the Duke asked.

She turned her head to look at him as if she could not help and he willed her to do so, and because they were sitting on the same level her eyes met his.

Time seemed to stand still and it was hard to breathe.

It was as if they were two people who met each other across eternity, and yet all the time Tempera was conscious of the gulf that lay between them, the gulf which held her Stepmother, her pretended identity, and, worst of all, the substitution of a fake for the Duke's picture.

"Tell me what is the matter?" he pleaded.

For one moment Tempera thought she must confess everything, and she felt too, although he did not move, that his arms reached out towards her.

She had only to make the smallest movement to be close against him, hiding her face against his shoulder.

Then with what was a superhuman effort she looked away; the spell was broken and she knew as it broke that there was a physical pain somewhere within her body.

With a convulsive movement she rose to her feet.

"I . . . I must go back . . . Your Grace," she said in a frightened voice that was somehow very young and very breathless. "I must beg Your Grace not to talk to me . . . not to come near me. I cannot . . . explain . . . but it is something which . . . must not . . . happen again."

The Duke did not move, and she looked down at his handsome face, the sunshine percolating through the leaves of the olive tree, casting little glimmers of gold on his hair.

Then with a sound that was almost a sob she turned and walked back the way she had come, climbing the twisting path which led back to the Château.

When she reached her own room, feeling it was hot and confining after the sunshine outside, Tempera flung herself down on her bed.

"Why? Why? Why does he make me feel like this?" she asked herself aloud.

She knew the answer, but at the same time she

dared not face it, dared not listen to her heart trying to tell her what her brain repudiated as being impossible.

* * *

When Lady Rothley returned from her drive with the Count she was glowing like a lovely jewel set against the light.

Since she had fallen in love her face had taken on a new beauty, and looking at her Tempera wondered how any man could resist anything so lovely.

"You were not here, Tempera, when the Count asked me to go driving with him," she said gaily, "but I found a light coat to cover my gown and Lady Barnard very sweetly lent me a long chiffon veil to tie over my hat."

As she spoke she flung her things down on the bed and walked across the room towards Tempera, crying rapturously:

"It was wonderful! Almost like flying in the sky or swimming in the sea. We sped along the road at least fifteen miles per hour! And the Count said one day he will take me out in his new racing-car, which does up to thirty! Think of it, Tempera! It is almost impossible to imagine such speed!"

"You had no right to go with the Count," Tempera said. The words seemed to be dragged from her.

"Nobody else asked me," Lady Rothley retorted, "and I wanted to go. It was such fun, Tempera—I have never been so happy!"

"*Belle-mère,* please be sensible. I know what you feel for this man. At the same time, suppose you accept his proposal and in five years, perhaps sooner, he is tired of you. . . . What then?"

"I do not know," Lady Rothley replied, "and I do not care! I love him, Tempera, and when he is there I cannot even see any other men, they simply do not exist!"

"And the Duke?"

"You will not believe me," Lady Rothley said, "but if the Duke asks me to marry him, I shall refuse."

"I cannot believe you," Tempera replied. "If he does propose marriage, you will accept."

"I will not! I will not!" Lady Rothley cried, banging her fists on the dressing-table. "I want to be with Vincenzo, and anyone else is a waste of time!"

"You have been asked to stay here for another week," Tempera said coldly, "then we have to go back to London. Have you asked the Count what his plans may be?"

"He was talking last night of returning to Italy," Lady Rothley said in a low voice, "but he was speaking to somebody else."

"He has not suggested coming to London?" Tempera persisted.

"No!"

"And do you think he is likely to?"

Lady Rothley put her hands up to her face.

"Do not torture me, Tempera, I know exactly what you are trying to say. I am not so stupid that I do not understand! But how can I resist being with him whenever I have the chance? To sit beside him in his motor-car is to be transported to Paradise! Oh, God, why do I feel like this? What am I to do?"

There was a silence, then weakly Tempera sat down on a chair.

"I do not know the answer to that, *Belle-mère*."

In fact, she told herself later, she did not know the answer to anything.

It was all too complicated, too difficult, and even while she was talking to her Stepmother she was haunted by the fact that below them the fake van Eyck was hanging on the wall just waiting to be discovered.

She knew, because her father had told her, that the Italians were very proud and strait-laced in matters concerning their family honour.

If there was a scandal over the picture and her Stepmother became involved in it, Tempera could not help thinking that she would damage her chances not only with the Duke but also with the Count.

'They are certain, in the first excitement of knowing it is a fake, to suspect me,' she thought.

It was obvious that suspicion would rest on her until she could clear herself, and it would not be difficult.

By the time she had revealed who she was and accused Lord Eustace, it would be paramount to proclaiming in headlines in the newspapers the deception they had imposed on their host, besides the fact that they were so poor that it was difficult for Lady Rothley to afford a proper lady's-maid.

Even her father would be involved, Tempera thought, because he had been unable to provide adequately for his widow and his daughter.

The whole thing would be like an avalanche where a tiny pebble once dislodged would dislodge another and yet another until half the mountain-side was hurtling downhill to destruction.

Such an avalanche, once launched, would utterly destroy her Stepmother in the Social World in which she wished to live; all that would remain for her in the future would be an obscurity which to her would be nothing but a living death.

"I have to save her," Tempera told herself, and at the same time thought frantically that she could see no possible way of doing so.

Her Stepmother rose from the dressing-table to begin taking off her clothes.

"I might as well rest while I have the chance," she said. "We are likely to be very late tonight."

"Why? Where are you going?" Tempera enquired.

"We are dining in Monte Carlo with the Grand Duke Boris of Russia. He has a huge party at the Hotel de Paris. I expect afterwards we will dance before going on to the Casino."

"Then you had better wear your white gown," Tempera said automatically.

She felt as if, while her lips were speaking, her brain was elsewhere, going round and round as if on a tread-mill, seeking as escape which did not present itself.

"Yes, the white will be very effective," Lady Rothley agreed, then she yawned and stretched herself.

"I want to go to sleep, Tempera, and when I wake up just to let everything happen without arguing with you or myself as to what is right or wrong."

"And that is what you shall do," Tempera said tenderly. "I will not say any more, *Belle-mère*. Just look beautiful and be happy."

Lady Rothley got into bed and Tempera pulled the curtains.

As she did so, she wondered how long her Stepmother's happiness would last.

* * *

Tempera walked down the passage to her own bed-room.

The Château was very quiet. She knew all the Duke's guests were resting and she longed to do downstairs and have one more look at the *Madonna in the Church*, just to make quite certain she was not mistaken.

But someone was sure to find her there, and anyway she thought it was quite unnecessary.

She had known with an unshakeable conviction this morning when she held the picture in her hands that it was a fake.

Although she had not her father's experience or what amounted to his clairvoyance where pictures were concerned, she was certain that there was no chance in this instance of her being proved wrong.

'Perhaps I had better tell the Duke the truth before he finds out,' she thought.

Then suddenly she saw quite clearly what she must do!

She need not tell the Duke or anybody else! The obvious course was for her to exchange the fake painting for the original which Lord Eustace had stolen.

Even as she thought of it she knew that here was the answer to everything—to her anxiety, to her fear of discovery, and most of all to the disaster of the Duke losing his picture.

She thought not only of herself and of her Step-mother, she thought of him.

She knew that, just as she would have felt in similar circumstances, it would be agonising for him to have something stolen which meant so much personally.

Tempera felt her heart begin to beat quicker, and now that the dark fog of uncertainty had lifted she could see daylight.

Unless she acted quickly Lord Eustace would dispose of the picture.

She tried to think what she herself would do in similar circumstances. She sat down on her bed and put her hands over her eyes, as if she forced herself to think clearly.

He had removed the genuine picture for the fake. Having done so, he would have taken the van Eyck upstairs with him to his bed-room. There he would have put it in a safe place where it would not be seen while he carried on as a guest in the house-party.

Even though he now had in his possession what he wanted, he would not leave precipitately, Tempera decided.

To do so would mean that when the theft was discovered his departure would obviously arouse sus-picion.

No, she thought, he would behave quite normally and continue his visit.

He might receive a telegram recalling him to England, but it was much more likely that he would leave at the end of the week or go to stay with other friends in the vicinity.

It was then that the picture would leave the Château.

In the meantime it was here, here in his bed-room, and what Tempera had to do was get hold of it.

She felt certain of one thing, and that was that Lord Eustace was not very knowledgeable about pic-tures.

His fake was a good one, but if he had seen it for the first time in a frame, it was doubtful whether he would have had the slightest suspicion it was not genuine.

Someone, however, like the Count or her father, or perhaps the Duke, would know instinctively without making tests that the picture was not a real van Eyck.

Tempera was sure that to Lord Eustace and his like the only interest in a picture was how much money it would fetch.

She suspected that he had a buyer already, perhaps a picture-dealer or just as likely one of the rich Americans who were only too ready to accept old Masters for their private Galleries and ask no questions as to how they were obtained.

"I have to get into Lord Eustace's room," Tempera told herself, "find where he had hidden the picture, and put the fake back in its place."

It was not going to be easy, she was aware of that, and if she was discovered while she was changing the pictures, she would be accused and doubtless convicted of the crime, however much she might protest her innocence.

Nobody would believe for a moment that, as her father's daughter, with her knowledge of painting and the fact that she had entered the Château disguised as a lady's-maid, she was not a criminal.

"It is a risk I shall have to take," Tempera said aloud.

The first difficulty was to find the right moment to search Lord Eustace's room.

It was helpful that, unlike the rest of the male guests, he did not have a personal valet.

Tempera had heard Miss Briggs and Miss Smith speaking of the valets who were in the house, and while Lord Holcombe and Sir William had each brought one with them, Lord Eustace was, she knew, looked after by one of the footmen.

When she remembered this she knew the exact moment when she must search Lord Eustace's room.

When the Duke and his guests dined in the Château, the staff ate before dinner was served in the Dining-Room; but when they dined out, the staff ate as soon as they had left.

This suited the Chef, who wanted a free evening when he had the chance, and Tempera knew that the moment the guests drove away from the front door the male staff would all troop into their own Dining-Room and sit down to a huge meal.

That was the moment, she thought, when she could slip up into the Tower and try to find the stolen van Eyck.

There was still half an hour before she need call her Stepmother and dress her for the evening which lay ahead.

In the meantime Tempera concentrated every nerve on trying to imagine where Lord Eustace would have hidden the picture.

He had been clever enough to steal one which was small. A canvas of only ten inches by eight and a half was very easy to conceal. Then she remembered her father telling her of a huge theft that had been perpetrated on one of the Galleries in Rome.

The thieves had cut a number of canvasses out of their frames and had actually escaped from the Gallery with them.

Their problem had then been to get them out of the city undetected.

Sir Francis had explained the various devices they had used.

"Of course the police had some idea of what the villains looked like," he said, "and they searched the luggage to be carried on every train for false-bottomed trunks and any bulky parcels which might contain a rolled-up canvas."

Tempera had listened with interest as her father had continued:

"One man had had a special walking-stick made into which a picture rolled very tightly could be inserted. Another walked with a lame leg, which sur-

prisingly proved to be the result of a canvas being
wound from knee to ankle."

Tempera laughed.

"Did they catch them all, Papa?"

"I think nearly every one," Sir Francis replied.
"But the most difficult to detect was a man who had a
landscape fastened to his bare back and another who
concealed a very much smaller picture inside his tall
hat."

He smiled as he added:

"He would have got away with it, but one of the
police-officers noticed that when a lady stopped him to
ask the way, he did not raise his hat!"

He laughed.

"Such an act of impoliteness cost him a ten-
thousand-pound piece of loot and seven years' impris-
onment!"

"I must look in Lord Eustace's hat," Tempera
told herself now.

She thought too that perhaps he might slip the
picture under the edge of the carpet or hide it behind
another picture on the wall in his room until he was
ready to leave with it.

"A good thief," Sir Francis had said, "seldom
uses a locked case—that is too obvious. And when it
comes to smuggling diamonds there is nothing more
effective than a hollowed-out book."

But Lord Eustace was not smuggling diamonds.
Nevertheless, the *Madonna in the Church* was so small
that it could easily be wrapped up in a newspaper or
slipped in the back of a photograph frame.

Mentally Tempera made a list of all the places she
must look, and she could only wonder almost despairingly whether she would have time for her search
before the servants finished dinner.

"You are very pensive, dearest," Lady Rothley
said as Tempera arranged her Stepmother's hair.

"I am making you look beautiful, *Belle-mère*."

"It is going to be a wonderful evening," Lady
Rothley said dreamily. "I can feel it in my bones."

An hour's sleep had swept away her depression and now she was glowing with excitement.

Tempera almost envied her as she stood up in her new white gown and looked as if she were stepping out of the Heavens on a white cloud.

"You will eclipse everybody at the party tonight," Tempera exclaimed.

As she spoke she wondered if it would be the last time her Stepmother would have the chance to do so.

Perhaps tomorrow or the next day they would be scuttling back to England in disgrace, to hide themselves in the house in Curzon Street and wonder what they would do in the future.

Then resolutely Tempera told herself that this must never happen. She must save them both, and in a strange way she felt certain that her father was helping and directing her.

It was almost as if he stood beside her, and when her Stepmother had gone downstairs and she waited to hear the carriage drive away she found herself praying as she had never prayed before.

"Help me, Papa, do not let me make a mistake. Show me where the picture is hidden."

She felt, because she loved the *Madonna in the Church* so much, that she would be able to pick up its vibrations and would therefore not waste too much time looking in a number of places in vain.

At the same time, it was hard to be certain of anything except that she was terribly nervous, her fingers were very cold, and she was trembling.

Even in her Stepmother's bed-room she could hear the voices and laughter of the house-party below her in the Sitting-Room.

They would be having a glass of champagne before they left, Tempera thought.

She could almost see her Stepmother looking exquisitely beautiful in her white gown, while Lady Holcombe's green eyes watched her jealously.

Lady Barnard would be kind and sweet, as she always was, trying to make everybody happy, while the

Count would undoubtedly be looking at *Belle-mère*
with his dark, eloquent eyes, and perhaps already paying her extravagant compliments which would sound
utterly sincere.

And what would the Duke be doing?

The question seemed almost to flash into Tempera's mind in letters of fire.

Would he too be admiring her Stepmother? Would
he be vying with the Count for a smile from her lips
and a warm look from her blue eyes?

Somewhere deep in her breast Tempera had a
pain that was almost like the stab of a dagger.

"I am jealous!" she told herself honestly. "How
can I be so absurd, so foolish, as to be jealous of
Belle-mère?"

She could see herself reflected in the mirror, see
her plain black gown, her pale face framed by her dark
hair.

Who was likely to look at her, she thought, when
her Stepmother glowed like the sun itself . . . a sun gold
and glorious, as Turner painted it?

She thought she could distinguish the Duke's
voice, and although she tried to think it was her imagination, the pain was still there. She forced herself
to think of what she had to do.

It was for his sake as well as for her own and her
Stepmother's.

How could she bear him to lose something he
treasured? How could a picture which spoke to him in
a way which only he could understand pass into alien
hands which would be concerned only with its worth
in terms of money rather than what its beauty meant to
the heart.

"I will save it! I have to!" Tempera murmured.

She thought the voices downstairs were fainter and
now she went to the door and opened it carefully.

She was right.

The party had moved into the hall. The ladies
were putting on their wraps and the gentlemen their
satin-lined cloaks.

She could hear the Duke's voice speaking distinctly and the rest were listening to him.

"Sir William, will you and your wife go in the first carriage," he was saying, "and take Eustace with you? And, Count, I am giving you a special treat. You shall escort Lady Rothley in the Brougham, and will you pick up the Lillingtons, to whom I have promised a lift, when you reach their Villa at Eze?"

"I shall be delighted!" the Count replied.

"How can the Duke send *Belle-mère* alone with the Count if it is for only a short distance?" Tempera questioned indignantly.

But she knew that her Stepmother would be only too delighted and there was no need even to guess what the Count's reaction would be.

"And, George," the Duke was continuing to Lord Holcombe, "you and I will play escort to your lovely wife."

Tempera guessed that Lady Holcombe would be delighted to drive with the Duke and would feel in some way that it was a score over her rival.

Having listened to their host's instructions, there was chatter and laughter again and Tempera could hear the party moving towards the front door. After a few moments the first carriage was driving away.

She waited, still with the door ajar.

The Brougham left, then the third carriage came to the door.

"Good-night, Bates," she heard the Duke say to the Butler.

"Good-night, M'Lord."

The footmen closed the carriage doors and Tempera could hear the horses moving over the gravel of the drive.

The footmen came back into the hall.

"We'll eat first," Bates said in his pontifical voice, "and clear the table afterwards."

"I was hoping you'd say that, Mr. Bates," one of the footmen remarked. "I'm feeling downright peckish!"

Another man joked about people being greedy,

and their voices and the sound of their footsteps died
away as they walked down the corridor which led to
the kitchen-quarters.

This was the moment for which Tempera had been
waiting.

She knew that Miss Briggs and Miss Smith would
be having their meal at the same time, and they would
not be inquisitive about her absence for the simple reason that she was often late and they much preferred to
gossip without her.

She stepped out onto the landing, shutting her
Stepmother's door, and hurried over the thick carpet
towards the flight of stairs which led up to the Tower.

She reached it, glanced down the hall to make
certain there was still nobody about, then ran up the
stairs which led to Lord Eustace's room.

The Tower room had three windows which, as
the Duke had said, provided the most spectacular view
in the whole Château. But for the moment Tempera
was not interested in views.

Everything had been tidied by the footman after
Lord Eustace had gone down to dinner, and she
guessed it would be a waste of time searching in the
chest-of-drawers to which the man-servant had access
or in the suits hanging in the wardrobe.

Lord Eustace obviously had few personal possessions with him.

There was no photograph in a frame, as she had
half-hoped, and the pigskin stud-box and the leather
flat holders for his razors were not large enough to
conceal even a small picture.

Quickly her eyes took in the ivory-handled
brushes in front of the mirror, and there was nothing of
any importance on the wash-hand-stand.

She hastily turned over several books which lay on
a bed-side table, but realised they were not the special
property of Lord Eustace, having the Duke's book-plate
inside them.

The pictures in the room were another place for

concealment and Tempera looked behind each one. It would have been easy to fix the van Eyck in the back of a frame, but there was nothing there.

She considered the carpet but found that it was fitted against the skirting board; the rugs which covered it were loose and were, she suspected, moved every morning by the conscientious French maids.

She began to feel frightened.

Supposing after all her plans she could not find the picture, or Lord Eustace had already taken it elsewhere?

Then she remembered her father's story of the man who had concealed in his hat a picture from the Gallery in Rome.

She opened the wardrobe.

In one corner next to a long row of Lord Eustace's highly polished shoes were two sturdy boxes in which gentlemen packed their tall hats when travelling.

They both came from Lock's in St. James's Street, as she might have expected, were of brown leather with a handle on the top, and were embossed with His Lordship's initials.

Tempera lifted the first one from the wardrobe, placed it on a chair, and undid the strap.

Inside, there was the polished top-hat which Lord Eustace wore in the daytime.

She took it out and looked inside, but saw at once that it contained nothing. She put it back and picked up the other hat-box.

This was empty, as she expected it would be, knowing that Lord Eustace was wearing his evening-hat at the moment.

Disappointed, she was just about to close the hat-box when an idea came to her.

The hat-boxes were lined inside with a satin padding.

Tempera realised it would be quite easy to conceal a picture as small as the van Eyck behind this.

She felt with her fingers where the padding joined

the leather. It seemed firmly secure. Then because the idea seemed to impress itself upon her, she opened again the hat-box she had already fastened.

She took out Lord Eustace's top-hat and again felt with her fingers round the edge of the lining.

For a moment she was disappointed, until she realised that it was not joined with stitching as the other case was but undoubtedly had been glued.

She pulled it away, while her heart seemed almost to stop with excitement.

Slipping her fingers down between the lining and the outside of the box, she felt something there.

It was only a question of seconds before she pulled it out with an exclamation of excitement she could not contain.

Then, holding the canvas in her hand, she stared at it in astonishment!

It was not van Eyck's *Madonna in the Church*, which she had expected to see, but the *Portrait of a Young Girl*, painted by Petrus Cristus.

She put it down on a chair and felt further round the hat-box.

Three minutes later she had in front of her not only the Petrus Cristus portrait and the *Madonna in the Church* by van Eyck, but the wooden panel of *St. George and the Dragon* painted by Raphael, which was under the lining of the flat-topped oval-shaped leather hat-box.

They were all small pictures which could be concealed without difficulty.

Tempera drew in her breath.

This was a haul she had not expected. At the same time, she realised warily that it was going to take her much longer to change all the pictures over and to put the fakes back in the hat-box so that Lord Eustace would not realise a substitution had taken place.

She could only pray she would have the opportunity to enter the Duke's room before the party returned from Monte Carlo.

She was well aware that she would have to wait until the servants had all gone to bed and she would also have to evade the notice of the night-footman who was on duty until everybody had returned.

'It is going to be difficult,' Tempera thought.

At the same time, she was so elated at finding what she sought that every other difficulty seemed to shrink into insignificance.

She put Lord Eustace's top-hat back into its box, fastened the straps, and replaced both boxes in the bottom of the wardrobe.

Then she closed the doors and picked up the pictures from the chair where she had laid them.

As she took up the *Madonna in the Church* she felt the beauty of it thrill her.

Even in the fading twilight it seemed to sparkle and come alive with a spiritual beauty which no fake, however skilful, could ever emulate.

"I have saved you!" Tempera whispered in her heart. "I have saved you because I am sure you called to me to do so. You told me what had happened and no fake could ever speak to me as you do."

She smiled down at the little picture and almost felt as if the Christ-child in the Madonna's arms blessed her.

Then, slipping the three pictures under her arm so that if she did meet anyone in the passages they could not see what she was carrying, she opened the door of Lord Eustace's room.

She stepped outside and closed the door very gently behind her. Then she hurried towards the landing, too excited to think of anything except that she had won!

She had been as clever as any policeman might be, and at least the first step of her appointed task was completed.

She had almost reached the landing when suddenly, unexpectedly and without any warning, she saw three people in front of her.

She stopped still, and although one hand went out to steady the pictures under her arm, she did not remove them.

Then, incredibly, she saw the Duke looking at her and realised that he and Lord Holcombe supported between them the sagging figure of Lady Holcombe!

Their arms were round her and Lord Holcombe was with his free hand opening the door of Lady Holcombe's room, which was just at the bottom of the steps leading up to the Tower.

Tempera stood as if turned to stone.

The look of astonishment and surprise on the Duke's face as he first saw her suddenly changed to a very different expression.

It was one of such contempt and disgust that she felt as if he had struck her.

As she stood staring at him, unable to move, he turned away to help carry Lady Holcombe into the bed-room.

Chapter Six

Tempera stood in her bed-room but found it impossible to think.

She felt as if someone had hit her on the head with a hammer and her brain had ceased to function.

Then slowly, as if she moved in a dream, she took the three pictures from under her arm and set them on her dressing-table.

Even the colours and the beauty of the *Madonna in the Church* meant nothing and all she could see was the expression on the Duke's face as he saw her standing on the stairs which led to the Tower.

She knew only too well what he had thought, and the horror of it was inescapable.

"How could he think I am capable of such behaviour?" she asked herself.

But she knew there could be no other reasonable explanation of her going to Lord Eustace's room, whether he was there or not.

It was unthinkable for a servant in attendance on a visiting Lady to be found entering the bed-room of a bachelor in the party, especially one with Lord Eustace's reputation.

The Duke, Tempera was sure, was well aware of his character, and he would find no excuse for her nor would he be prepared to give her the benefit of the doubt.

Tempera put her hands up to her face, feeling it must be burning with humiliation; but she could only feel the cold of her fingers, which seemed to her almost like those of a skeleton.

She felt as if everything beautiful, everything she believed in, everything in which she had faith, had crashed round her. She knew that she had lost not only the Duke's interest in her but also her own pride.

She disliked Lord Eustace so violently that to be connected with him in any way was degrading to her self-respect.

But that the Duke should think her capable of liking such a man and associating with him was, Tempera thought, to humble her into the dust so that she felt as if she would never be able to raise her head again.

She wanted more than she had ever wanted anything in her whole life to find the Duke immediately, to show him the pictures and explain why she had been in Lord Eustace's room.

Then, as she knew that this was the one thing she could not do, she felt as if her whole world had come to an end.

She did not have to ask herself now why she felt so distressed or why the condemnation on the Duke's face had been so devastating.

She knew in her heart, in her mind, and in her very soul that she loved him.

She had loved him, she thought, ever since the first moment she had seen him, as soon as he had spoken to her.

His deep voice had somehow had the power to stir her as she had never been stirred before, and every time they met she had fallen more and more in love.

And yet, because of her loyalty to her Stepmother and because she was proud, she had not admitted it to herself.

But it had been there, increasing every day until, when they sat together in the moonlight and looked out over the sea, she had felt as if her whole being was a part of his and they were indivisible.

"I love him! I love him!" she murmured as she walked despairingly about her room, unable to keep still.

It was a physical as well as a mental agony to know what he was thinking, to feel almost as if his disgust made her unclean.

'And that is what I would be if it were the truth,' she thought hopelessly.

She knew now that her efforts to avoid the Duke had really been an instinct of self-preservation against a love so deep, so violent, so overpowering that it completely possessed her.

She had always known that somewhere in the world there must be a man for whom she could feel as she felt now, and when she found him it would not matter if he was a Duke or a pauper.

All that would concern her was that he was the second half of herself and she was complete only because he was there.

'He will not only despise me, he will also hate me!' she thought.

She knew this was true because they had together known the ecstasy of beauty and felt it vibrate within them.

Inexperienced though she was, Tempera realised that it had been an ecstasy that was vouchsafed to few men and women.

Yet they had known it, just as they had found they were moved in the same way by the beauty of the *Madonna in the Church*.

"What can I . . . do? How can I . . . explain to him? How will he ever . . . know he is wrong?" Tempera asked.

But she knew there were no answers to her questions and there never would be.

She looked at the pictures lying on her dressing-table and thought that she was now in an even worse predicament than she had anticipated.

Whatever the reason for the return of the Duke with Lord and Lady Holcombe to the Château, it was unlikely they would leave it again this evening.

In which case it might be impossible for her to switch the pictures as she had intended.

Then what should she do with them?

She was standing at the window, staring out into the darkness, when there was a knock at the door.

Tempera started and instinctively her hands went to her breast. . . .

"C-come in!"

Her voice sounded strange even to herself.

But when the door opened it was Miss Smith who stood there.

"I thought you would like to know, Miss Riley, that there's been an accident to Lady Holcombe."

"What has . . . h-happened?" Tempera managed to ask.

"Apparently as they were driving along the Corniche Road towards Monte Carlo a dray driven by a drunken or at any rate an incompetent driver, came out of a side-turning. Only by extremely good driving did the coachman prevent what might have been a very dangerous accident!"

"But . . . Her Ladyship . . . is hurt?" Tempera asked.

"She bumped her head when the carriage stopped suddenly," Miss Smith explained. "I believe she has a slight cut, but it is the shock that has upset her, and Miss Briggs tells me she has a splitting head-ache."

Miss Smith was obviously delighted to be the bearer of news whether good or bad.

"I often think these roads are extremely dangerous," she went on. "They're far too narrow, for one thing, and if the carriage had overturned there could have been a very different story to tell!"

"Yes . . . there would," Tempera agreed.

It was a tremendous effort to force herself to concentrate on what Miss Smith was saying, and while she was listening she was suddenly conscious that the three pictures which she had brought from Lord Eustace's room were lying on her dressing-table.

She took an anxious glance at them but realised with relief that Miss Smith was not interested in pictures.

"This puts paid to His Lordship attending the party tonight," she was saying, "but I'm wondering if His Grace'll go out again. He never cares much for parties, I understand, so he may find it a good excuse to cry off."

"I expect then they will have their dinner here," Tempera said, wondering how this would affect her plans.

"I expect so," Miss Smith agreed. "It's lucky your Lady wasn't in the carriage, and of course my Lady, too. They should be in Monte Carlo by this time."

She yawned.

"I must say, I rather envy Miss Briggs. She'll have an early night for once."

"Yes ... of course," Tempera agreed. "Is there anything I can do to help Her Ladyship?"

"I expect Miss Briggs has everthing she needs," Miss Smith replied. "She just rushed in to get a bottle of Eau de Cologne and told me what had happened. I am wondering what had occurred when one of the footmen came bounding up to say she was wanted."

She opened the door to leave the room and added as she did so:

"It just shows, Miss Riley, as I've said so often, we're never off duty. Just when we think we're in for a quiet evening something like this happens. I often says to myself that it's a dog's life, and that's what it is!"

She did not wait for an answer, but left Tempera alone.

It was hard for her to think of anything but the Duke downstairs.

She had an overpowering urge to go down to him, hand him the pictures, and make him realise that she had not behaved as he thought, but was in fact saving some of his most treasured possessions.

But she knew that if she did that, it was inevitable that he would learn her true identity.

He was bound to take action against Lord Eustace, and it would only be her word against his that the pictures were concealed in his hat-box.

The Count would be told about the attempted theft and a long-drawn-out investigation as to the identity of the forger might begin.

People like her father in the Art World had always been on the look-out for the men who could forge so skilfully that at times they could even deceive the experts.

The Count, who was of great consequence in Italy, would be only too pleased to lay one of these counterfeiters by the heels, and if the Duke decided to prosecute Lord Eustace, the situation would be even worse.

Then not only the gossips of Monte Carlo but the whole world would learn that Lady Rothley had passed her Stepdaughter off as a lady's-maid.

"It is impossible! Quite . . . impossible!" Tempera exclaimed.

But every nerve in her body cried out that she should exonerate herself in the Duke's eyes.

She felt as if her love must somehow communicate itself to him, and yet she knew that the sight of her outside Lord Eustace's room had erected a barrier between them that was insurmountable.

Never again would he come in search of her, whether she was hiding down by the ravine or sitting in the moonlight overlooking the sea.

Never again would he be interested in her pictures or wish to see them.

Never again would he want to talk to her in a manner which made her remember and repeat to herself in the darkness of the night every word he had said.

"If this is love, it is an agony beyond expression," Tempera told herself, "because it brings me only a darkness so impenetrable that I can never escape from it."

She thought that all her life she would be lonely and desolate, with nothing to remember save those few moments when she had been as close to the Duke as if he had held her in his arms.

"Why did I leave him when I could have stayed longer with him?" she asked herself now.

She remembered how she had run back to the Château after they had been together in the moonlight, and realised she had run away not from him but from her own feelings.

"Oh, God, what shall I do?" she prayed without hope, and felt that even her prayers were lost in the misery of her despair.

After a while she put the three pictures in the drawer of her dressing-table and went to her Stepmother's room to await her return.

It was impossible to think coherently but she forced herself to make a plan.

Somewhere downstairs the Duke was sitting, perhaps alone or with Lord Holcombe, and her only chance of changing the pictures would be when everybody had gone to bed.

'Once that is done,' she thought, 'I must keep out of sight of the Duke and if necessary stay in my bedroom until it is time for us to return to England.'

It struck her that even if she got the chance of changing over the pictures as she intended, it would not be impossible to go back to Lord Eustace's room to replace the fakes.

There was a chance that she might be able to do that tomorrow, but if not, it was of no particular consequence.

It would be inconceivable for him to have further copies made quickly.

He must have planned this operation for a long time.

Tempera knew that the copies would have been made from other copies of the original pictures.

All van Eyck's works were known and catalogued and it was possible to buy quite good reproductions in an Art Shop.

But that was not to say that the really superlative

fakes which Lord Eustace had substituted for the original pictures were easily obtainable.

"If I destroy the fakes in some way it will be a long time before Lord Eustace can get some more done, get another invitation to stay in the Château, and take away the originals," Tempera told herself.

It was reaching the end of the season and she was certain of one thing: it would be at least a year before he could make another attempt to steal the pictures from the Duke's collection.

This was somehow reassuring, and she thought that after all the only important thing she had to do was to replace the originals in their frames.

It was certainly a far less complicated operation than she had planned originally, and when Lord Eustace discovered his loss there would be nothing he could do about it.

"At least I will have saved three Masterpieces for the future," Tempera murmured, and added beneath her breath: "and for the Duke!"

It was the one thing she could do for him, whatever his feelings for her; the one way in which she could express her love, even though he would never know it.

She lay down on her Stepmother's bed but found it impossible to sleep.

Her brain kept going over and over what she had to do, and when she shut her eyes all she could see was the expression of astonishment on the Duke's face being replaced by one of contempt.

"I am not like that!" she longed to cry aloud into the darkness.

But the control she had always kept over herself made her lie silent and suffering until many hours later she heard her Stepmother's voice coming up the stairs.

She was rather slow in getting off the bed, so she did not hear what Lady Rothley was saying, although there was a lilt in her voice which was there only when she was feeling gay and excited.

Tempera opened the door, and as she came into

the room her Stepmother put her arms round her and hugged her.

"Oh, Tempera, Tempera!" she cried. "It is so wonderful and I am so happy! I am engaged! Congratulate me, dearest! I can hardly believe it is true!"

"The Count has asked you to marry him?"

"He has not asked me, he has told me that I have to because he cannot live without me!" Lady Rothley replied. "I am the luckiest, most fortunate woman in the whole world!"

She flung her wrap down on the chair to stand staring at herself in the long mirror which ornamented the front of the wardrobe.

"Is this really me?" she asked in a wondering voice. "Can it be true that I am in love, as I never thought it possible to be, with the most wonderful man in the world?"

"Oh, *Belle-mère, Belle-mère!* I am so happy for you!" Tempera cried.

Lady Rothley turned to hug her again.

"You thought he would not ask me," she said, "but he has! He wants me to be his wife, and we are leaving for Italy the day after tomorrow so that he can present me to his family."

"You will be married there?"

"That is what he plans, and I am happy to leave everything in his hands. All I want to do is to please him!"

Lady Rothley gave a deep sigh of contentment.

"He is so masterful, so completely sure of what he wants and determined to have it. That is what I love about him."

She sat down at her dressing-table as she went on:

"He says that he fell in love with me the moment he saw me, and that he has spent all his life looking for someone as beautiful as me!"

"It all sounds too wonderful!" Tempera said.

"It is!" Lady Rothley agreed. "It is so lucky we came here, but how horrifying it would have been if I had accepted the Duke before I met Vincenzo."

Tempera did not reply and after a moment her Stepmother said:

"You must not think, dearest, that I shall forget you because I am to be married. You must go back to England and then I will send for you and you will be able to meet Vincenzo as your father's daughter."

"I would not wish to be an encumbrance upon you, *Belle-mère*," Tempera said humbly.

"You could never be that!" Lady Rothley replied with a smile. "I know that it is partially due to your making me look so beautiful that Vincenzo fell in love with me."

She gave another deep sigh.

"Thank goodness we spent that money at Lucille's before we came here. Supposing he had not noticed me?"

"It was your face he looked at, not your clothes."

"That sounds all right in a story-book," Lady Rothley said, "but you know as well as I do that clothes are terribly important. If I had gone to the Casino in any old rag, I would not have created a sensation and so made Vincenzo jealous because so many men were paying attention to me."

"Papa was very fond of the Count," Tempera said quietly, "and I think, *Belle-mère,* he would be pleased to know of your happiness."

"Perhaps he does know," Lady Rothley answered, "and I am glad Vincenzo was a friend of dear Francis. I am lucky, very lucky, to have had two such wonderful men in my life."

Tempera bent and kissed her Stepmother's cheek. Then she helped her to undress and get into bed.

"Call me early tomorrow morning," Lady Rothley said as she turned out the lights. "I could not bear to miss a moment of the time when I might be with Vincenzo."

Tempera went to her own room.

Now at last her Stepmother was safe for the future and happier than Tempera had ever seen her.

But as far as she herself was concerned there was no happy ending, no light at the end of her dark tunnel.

She could not help thinking that if it were not for Lord Eustace, she might no longer be feeling guilty about the interest the Duke was taking in her—or had it only been in her paintings?

There would be no reason to run away from him or be afraid that any further interest might damage her Stepmother's chances.

She could have talked to him naturally as he talked to her, but all that was finished! He would never want to see her again and the sooner she left the Château the better.

She realised that tomorrow she would have to plan very carefully if the Count was not to meet her before he and *Belle-mère* set off for Italy, and that she must think of an excuse for her Stepmother as to why her maid would not travel with her.

Perhaps if she packed everything ready, she might be able to slip away on an afternoon or evening train to London.

Her whole being cried out at the thought of leaving the Duke behind, of going back to the loneliness of the house in Curzon Street with only old Agnes for company.

And when her Stepmother sent for her, what would be the point of her going to Italy and meeting new people, new men, or trying to find new interests, when part of her—the part that mattered—would have been left behind with the Duke here in the South of France?

She knew that spiritually she would never meet another man who could make her feel as the Duke had done.

She knew that physically she would never meet another man who was as attractive or who made her heart leap at the sound of his voice.

"The picture of myself which I shall present to

the world in the future will always be a fake," Tempera told herself whimsically. "The real me will be dead and no-one will ever resuscitate it."

She had left the door of her bed-room a little open and now, although it was round the corner, she could hear people and voices coming up the stairs.

She realised that Sir William and Lady Barnard had returned and the Duke was with them, telling them what had happened to Lady Holcombe.

"I am so sorry," Lady Barnard was saying in her sweet voice, "what a terrible thing to happen! Poor Rosie! I would go and commiserate with her, but I expect she will be asleep."

"I am sure she will be," the Duke answered, "and George retired over an hour ago."

"Then I must keep my condolences until the morning," Lady Barnard said. "She missed such a delightful party, and so did you, Velde."

"It was too late after the accident for me to start off again for Monte Carlo," the Duke replied. "I will send His Serene Highness my apologies in the morning."

"It was a very glamorous party," Lady Barnard said, "and everybody of any importance was there. Lady Rothley looked radiant!"

"I am sure she will want to tell you the reason why in the morning," the Duke replied.

"Do you mean . . . ?" Lady Barnard was obviously curious.

"Lady Rothley has made the Count very happy," the Duke replied. "I have just been congratulating them."

"Oh, how delightful!" Lady Barnard exclaimed. "Did you hear that, William? Lady Rothley is engaged to that attractive Count Vincenzo Caravargio. They certainly had eyes for no-one else tonight."

"A good-looking woman!" Sir William remarked.

"I expect you will be told all about it tomorrow," the Duke said. "Good-night, Lady Barnard, good-night, Sir William."

Tempera heard the Barnards go into their room on the other side of Lady Rothley's and close the door.

Now, she thought, she had to wait for the three men to come to bed, then the way would be clear for her to go downstairs.

She did not have to wait long before she heard the Duke and the Count.

They were talking as they walked up the stairs side by side, and there was the sound of two doors shutting. But she realised that Lord Eustace had not been with them.

It must have been half an hour later before she heard him come up the stairs, alone, and she fancied, although she might have been mistaken, that his footsteps were heavy, as if he was either tired or had been drinking.

Now she knew that with everyone back in the Château the night-footman in the hall would go to bed.

She moved to the window and saw that the moon was shining silver over the valley behind the Château and the light was almost as clear as day, certainly as clear as it would be in the very early morning.

Tempera took the pictures from the drawer in her dressing-table and carried them to the window.

She could see their beauty in the moonlight and thought as she had thought before that it would be impossible for anyone to copy adequately the *Madonna in the Church*.

As always, the spiritual quality of the painting seemed to stir her soul, and yet what she felt was tinged with a sadness which only added to the misery and depression she already felt.

Never again would she hold anything so exquisite in her hands, never again would she be able to think of this jewel without remembering the Duke.

She had thought that the Christ-child blessed her, but instead the possession of it even for a few hours had brought her the greatest unhappiness she could ever experience.

However, because she loved the Duke, she was

glad that such a treasure would be returned to his keeping.

"Take care of him," she whispered to the Madonna in the picture, "watch over him, keep him free from harm, and bring him happiness in his life."

It was the most unselfish prayer she could possibly make, yet it came from her heart, and she knew that even though she could not share it with him, because she loved the Duke she wanted him to be happy.

Perhaps one day he would find love as her Stepmother had.

Perhaps one day he would know the ecstasy and the wonder of loving and being loved, while he would never know that the maid-servant whom he despised would love him until the day she died.

Tempera felt the tears come into her eyes, but fiercely she forced them away. Turning from the window, still carrying the three pictures in her hands, she went to the door to listen.

There was only the quiet of utter silence, and moving stealthily, afraid that even through the thick carpet a floor-board might creak, she moved along the passage and holding on to the bannister began to descend the stairs.

The light was very faint in the hall because although the windows were long and high the curtains which covered them were heavy so that the moonlight could not percolate through them.

In the Sitting-Room the curtains were of silk, and from the windows which covered almost the whole side of the room there was a silver glow.

Tempera moved quickly into the Duke's room.

She thought as she entered that the atmosphere was redolent of him and his personality.

It seemed to strike her as it had never done before and she stood for a moment, feeling that he had impressed himself so vividly upon the room that it was almost as if he were there waiting for her.

Then she told herself sharply that there was no time to be lost.

She went to the window and very slowly, so that they made no sound, she drew back the curtains to let in the moonlight.

It poured in in a silver flood, touching the pictures on the walls with a magic light, and glimmering on the ink-pot on the desk against which she had propped her painting.

One ray seemed to spotlight the picture of the angel from Leonardo da Vinci's Masterpiece.

Tense though she was, Tempera could not help wondering whether just sometimes, when the Duke looked up from his desk and his eyes alighted on the angel opposite him, he would think of her.

There was no reason to believe that he had ever connected her in any way with the portrait, and yet she knew, as her father had seen, that the shape of her face was the same as that of the angel, her eyes had the same slant, and her lips when she smiled had the same curve.

'If it does remind him of me,' she thought unhappily, 'he will either dismiss the thought from his mind or perhaps even dispose of the picture. To him I am not an angel but a fallen woman! And there will be no-one to tell him that he is wrong.'

She put the three pictures down on the Duke's desk and went to the wall to lift down the frame which contained the fake *Madonna in the Church*.

By the light of the moon it was easy to see exactly how the canvas fitted into the frame, and Lord Eustace had replaced the nails in the same position as he must have found them.

It was therefore not hard to pull them out, but Tempera had to lay the picture face downwards on the desk to do so.

Only one nail resisted the pressure of her fingers, so that she was obliged to use a gold paper-knife which lay beside the Duke's blotter.

It was easy then to lift out the fake picture and replace the original.

She pressed the nails back into place and knew they would have held more effectively if she had been able to tap them into place, but that would make a noise.

So she merely used the strength of her thumb and fingers, hoping that it would hold the canvas at least until Lord Eustace had left the Château.

When she had finished as best she could, she picked up the picture and carried it from the desk to the wall.

Just for one moment she stared down at it in the moonlight, feeling once again that it spoke to her as it had before.

The sunlight shining through the Gothic windows sparkled on the precious stones on the Madonna's crown and seemed to hold a special message of hope, but for her Tempera knew it was only an illusion.

There could be no hope for her, no light in her darkness, and the picture would in the future speak only to the Duke.

"Take care of him," she prayed again.

As she reached out to place the picture back on the wall she heard the door at the further end of the room open, and she turned her head.

Someone entered, and for a moment, because the moonlight did not percolate so far, she could not see who it was.

Then as a man advanced towards her she saw with a frightened leap of her heart that it was Lord Eustace.

"So you are the one who has been interfering!" he said.

There was a sharpness and venom in his voice that made her instinctively take a step backwards, still holding the picture in her hands.

"Who are you and what the devil are you doing here in this house?" he asked.

He seemed almost to snarl the words at her, and now to her surprise Tempera found her voice and an anger which for the moment overcame her fear.

"Did you really believe that your fakes would be convincing to anyone who understands Art?" she enquired.

"How did you know they were fakes?"

"I used my eyes," Tempera replied, "but I did not believe that any man of your rank would behave in such a despicable and criminal manner."

"Is that what you call it?"

Lord Eustace had come near to Tempera and was standing looking down at her, but strangely enough she was not so afraid of him as she had been when he first appeared.

"I have put one picture back where it belongs," she said, "and now I intend to replace the others. You can take your fakes and hide them away in your hat-box."

"Do you really think I will allow you to do this?" Lord Eustace asked.

He was still wearing the evening-clothes in which he had gone out to dinner. She thought that for some reason he must have been concerned about the pictures and had wanted to examine them before going to bed, and thus had discovered that they were missing.

"How can you stop me?" she asked, replying to his question. "If you make a scene over my behaviour, you will have to explain your own."

"That is true," Lord Eustace said. "You have put me in a very uncomfortable position, have you not— you bogus lady's-maid!"

"I hope I have taught you a lesson," Tempera retorted, "that your fakes are not good enough to deceive a connoisseur of paintings."

She looked up into Lord Eustace's face as she spoke and saw there a strange expression which was hard to describe.

She was certain it was not entirely one of frustration at being caught out, and it was certainly not embarrassment.

He was in fact looking at her calculatingly, and she thought that he intended to bribe her not to reveal what had occurred.

Unexpectedly he walked to the window and flung it open.

It was hot in the room, and the cool night air seemed to Tempera to relieve not only the heat but also her tension.

"I will change the other two pictures over now," she said to Lord Eustace, "and because I do not wish to be involved in this unpleasant scheme, I will say nothing to your host of your behaviour—I will leave it to your conscience."

"You are very brave," Lord Eustace sneered. "Supposing I raise the alarm and tell everybody that I caught you substituting fakes for the Duke's pictures?"

Tempera paused for a moment to think, but she had the answer.

"It will be quite easy for me to prove that I have never had enough money to get in touch with any forger and buy fake pictures," she said quietly. "Any accusation against me would involve the minutest investigation, as you are well aware, and it could be proved, I am quite certain, that I am not in the same need of money as you are."

"You think you have all the answers," Lord Eustace replied. "It is a pity that I have no time to listen to your life-story. It should be enlightening."

The way he spoke made Tempera look at him a little uncertainly. He reached out his hand and took the picture from her.

"You will not need this where you are going," he said.

He put it down on the nearest chair.

Then before Tempera realised what was happening, before she could try to struggle or run away, he had placed his hand roughly over her mouth, and at the same time put his other arm round and lifted her off her feet.

"Dead men tell no tales," he said, and now there was a jeering note in his voice, "and a dead lady's-maid will not evoke even a ripple of interest!"

It was then that Tempera realised what he was about to do.

She began to struggle violently and frantically, striving at the same time to scream, but it was impossible.

He was very strong, and his hand covering her mouth forced back her head at an angle which rendered her helpless.

She struck at him with her hands but knew the impact against his chest and shoulders was ineffective, and all the time relentlessly he was carrying her towards the open window.

"This should teach you not to interfere in other people's concerns," he said mockingly.

She felt the window-ledge hard against her body as he pushed her head outside, turning her face downwards.

She saw in one terrifying glance the sheer precipice beneath her, the drop which would land her far below on the rocks.

This was utter destruction. This was death.

She stretched out her arms to clutch the sides of the window, holding frantically on to the frame, knowing as Lord Eustace took his hand from her mouth to loosen her grip that she was as ineffectual and helpless as a doll.

With what she thought was her last breath she screamed, but only a ghost-like sound came from between her lips.

Then as he pulled away her clutching fingers, as she felt him tip her further out the window, there was a sudden noise of voices.

Even as Tempera waited to fall and could almost feel the pain of it, hands were on her waist, dragging her back.

For a moment everything spun dizzily round her and she felt as if her heart stopped beating.

Then she was close in someone's arms and she knew who unbelievably, incredibly, at the very last moment had saved her.

But she was too shaken and too frightened for the

moment to be aware of anything except that she was not to die and the rocks were no longer there beneath her.

Someone spoke above her head, but she could not understand what was being said; she only knew that she had been saved and who had saved her.

She was trembling, her eyes were closed, and her face was buried against the Duke's shoulder as he lifted her in his arms.

She felt him carry her into the Sitting-Room to set her down on the sofa, but she held on to him frantically.

She could not let him go, could not be sure that death was not waiting for her, and that even now she would not fall to be battered to death on the rocks at the bottom of the precipice.

"It is all right," she heard him say. "It is all right. You are safe!"

It was then, as if in the utter relief of knowing she did not have to die, that the tears came and she began to cry.

She felt his arms tighten and he said:

"You are safe, my darling, you are safe, no-one shall ever hurt you again!"

She thought she must be dreaming and it was part of her imagination, but she felt his lips against her forehead and raised her face with the tears running down her cheeks, to look up at him.

"How could you have done anything so dangerous as to try to put the pictures back?" the Duke asked.

"Y-you . . . knew they had . . . gone?"

It was hard to recognise her own voice—it was so hoarse—and she was still trembling with fear.

"I knew it before I went out to dinner tonight," the Duke answered. "The Count realised as soon as he looked at the Raphael that it was a fake."

"I did not . . . know Lord Eustace had . . . taken that one until I . . . f-found them in his . . . room," Tempera said.

"Why did you not come at once and tell me what you had discovered?" the Duke asked. "My precious,

I would not have had you involved in anything like this."

Tempera's eyes, in the moonlight, still misty with tears, looked up into his.

"Wh . . . what are you . . . saying to . . . me?" she asked.

The Duke smiled.

"Do I really need to tell you that I have loved you from the first moment I saw you? You are Leonardo da Vinci's angel I have been trying to find all my life."

Tempera drew in her breath.

"You . . . did think . . . there was a . . . resemblance?" she stammered.

"I saw it the first time I found you in the garden."

He turned his head as he spoke, as if to look behind him, and Tempera realised that the connecting door between the Sitting-Room and the room from which he had rescued her was closed.

As if he felt an explanation was necessary the Duke said:

"We can leave Lord Eustace to the Count. All I am concerned about is you, my precious one."

Then before Tempera could reply, before she could really understand what was happening, the Duke bent his head and his lips took possession of hers.

For a moment she felt only surprise; then, like the feeling she had had for the *Madonna in the Church,* the beauty and wonder of it drew her soul from her body so that it became his.

He drew her closer and closer until it was impossible to think; she could only feel.

The fear, the terror, the world itself disappeared and there was only the Duke, the closeness of him, and a glory that came from the moonlight which enveloped them both.

It was so spiritual, so perfect that Tempera felt she must have died and was now in Heaven.

This was what she had longed for. This was love as she had always known it would be.

This was a happiness which was a light to the heart.

Chapter Seven

Tempera walked through the gardens of the Villa Caravargio in Rome, moving between the exquisite statuary posed against the cypress trees.

She was wearing a gown of madonna blue chiffon which might have stepped from the pictures of a Master-painter and which toned in with the flowers which grew in profusion over the stone balustrade and round the plinths of the statues.

It was the moment when the sun was going down and a golden light hovered above Rome and at the same time seemed to rise from it.

As she reached the part of the garden from which there was one of the finest views in all the world, she could see below her the whole city laid out like a child's toy. The Dome of St. Peter's was silhouetted against the golden sky.

Gradually an upsurge of red light spread in the west and moved up to blend with the dark blue of the dying summer day.

She responded to the beauty of it, while at the same time her heart was vibrating to the knowledge that in a short while, perhaps in a few minutes, the Duke would have arrived from France and be with her.

She had felt she could not bear to meet him inside the Villa but must be alone when he came to her, surrounded by the loveliness that she knew would be a part of their lives.

It seemed impossible to believe that only a week ago she had escaped death by seconds and had been pulled back from destruction to know an almost unearthly happiness in the Duke's arms.

She relived in her mind the precious memory of how he had kissed her and she felt that no-one could experience such ecstasy and not die at the wonder of it.

Then he had asked, his voice curiously unsteady:

"When will you marry me, my darling?"

It was at that moment for the first time since he had saved her that she came back to the reality of the situation.

"Y-you cannot . . . you must not . . . it is wrong . . ." she began to stammer incoherently.

He understood what she was trying to say and smiled.

"I should be proud and very honoured to marry the daughter of my father's friend, Sir Francis Rothley,"

"You . . . knew?"

He smiled and pulled her closer to him.

"When I saw you first in the garden and found incredibly that you were the Leonardo da Vinci angel I had been trying to find all my life, I fell in love with you, my sweet."

He paused to say:

"No—that is not true. I have loved you since I was nine years old, but that is a story I will tell you later."

Tempera made a little sound and he went on:

"But I knew that you were mine, that you belonged to me, that nothing should keep us apart. That, my precious, was what I felt in my heart, but my brain made me behave a little more sensibly."

Tempera looked up at him wide-eyed, her head against his shoulder, and he continued:

"Because of my possessions, many of them as you know irreplaceable, I have a very efficient method of security."

He smiled as he continued:

"When I telegraphed London for information about Lady Rothley's lady's-maid, I was informed that she did not have one but that she was accompanied to the South of France by her Stepdaughter—Miss Tempera Rothley."

"So that was how you ... knew who I was really. . . ."

"Yes, my darling, that was how I knew, but because you wished it I let you continue with your deception."

"I did not tell ... you about the ... pictures," Tempera murmured, "because I thought it would ... harm *Belle-mère* for people to learn I was acting as her ... lady's-maid."

"That was understandable, except that it exposed you to a danger I cannot bear to think about."

She heard the throb in the Duke's voice and because it moved her she hid her face against him, whispering:

"I am ... safe now."

"As you always will be," the Duke replied. "I will never let you out of my sight, and if any man tries again to hurt you I will kill him!"

As if Lord Eustace was recalled to her mind by the violence of his words, Tempera looked towards the closed door.

"He will never harm you again," the Duke said.

"If there is an ... enquiry, people will know about ... me and it might ... damage *Belle-mère*."

"It is so like you, my lovely one, to think of everyone but yourself," the Duke said. "But I am sure the Count will find a solution. At the moment I can only think of your lips."

His mouth held her captive and it was impossible to think of anything but him.

The Count when he joined them was, Tempera learnt, prepared to deal with everything very effectively.

He kissed her on the cheek and said:

"From the position in which I find you in Velde's

arms I imagine I have to congratulate him as he has to congratulate me."

"I am so happy about *Belle-mère*."

"And I am happy about you," he answered. "It is everything your father would have wished for you."

He spoke so sincerely that Tempera found there were tears in her eyes as she replied:

"I am very, very . . . lucky!"

"You have taken the words out of my mouth," the Duke said. "I am the lucky one."

"I think we are all very fortunate people," the Count said, "but we have to be sensible: to create a scandal is unthinkable."

"What have you done with Eustace?" the Duke asked.

"I have told him to leave your house within the hour," the Count replied, "and that unless he journeys to South Africa to join his father you will take proceedings against him not only for theft but also for attempted murder!"

Tempera gave a little cry of protest, and the Count said:

"Do not be alarmed. I meant to frighten him and I have succeeded. He will do as I have suggested because he has no alternative."

"You are sure he will obey you?" the Duke asked.

"I am certain of it," the Count replied, and his voice was grim. "I have told Eustace that he is not to set foot in Europe for five years. I am certain these are not the first fake pictures he has substituted for originals. I will put in hand an immediate investigation."

"You see, my darling," the Duke said to Tempera, "I told you we could leave everything in Vincenzo's capable hands."

It was indeed the Count who had planned everything.

Lady Rothley and her lady's-maid had left the Château a day earlier than was first intended and were on the train for Italy by midday.

The Count accompanied them. Only when the

train had steamed out of the station did Tempera move from the Second Class compartment into which the Duke's servants had put her with the hand-luggage to join her Stepmother and the Count in their reserved carriage.

It was a journey that seemed to be brilliant with happiness: the Count and Lady Rothley were both radiant, and Tempera read over and over again the note which the Duke had given her before she left.

In it he expressed his love so eloquently that she almost felt as if he were beside her.

"Velde will join us in Italy as soon as he can leave his house-party without showing undue haste," the Count explained. "His excuse will be that he wishes to be at our wedding, and indeed we are very anxious that he should be there, and you, my dear Tempera, will be waiting for him."

The joy in Tempera's eyes told him what she thought of this arrangement.

She arrived in Rome looking rather drab because she had only the clothes she had brought from London.

Within twenty-four hours the chrysalis, as she told herself, was transformed into a butterfly.

The Count ordered the best dressmakers in Rome to come to the Villa and provided her with such an exquisite trousseau that she felt the Duke might find it impossible to recognise her.

When she protested at the Count's almost overwhelming generosity he laughed and said:

"It is part of my wedding-present to you, and may I say that I can never be grateful enough for your father's friendship and for your kindness and sweetness to my future wife."

If Tempera was ecstatically happy at the thought of her own future, she was equally sure that her Stepmother had found the one man who could make her happy.

The Count treated Lady Rothley not as a child, as her father had done, but as something so precious that he must protect her from everything that was harsh and ugly, disagreeable or disturbing.

"All you have to do, *mia bella,*" Tempera heard him say once, "is to look beautiful, so that you fill my eyes to the exclusion of all else."

"I am so happy, so terribly happy!" Lady Rothley said every night when she kissed Tempera good-night. "How could we ever guess, you and I, when we set off for the South of France that we were really embarking on a journey to Paradise?"

That, Tempera thought, was what it would be when she married the Duke, and now as she waited for him she could feel her heart beating faster because every second she drew nearer to the moment when they would be together.

The golden glow over the city of Rome had darkened as had the blue sky. High above the cypress trees the first evening star began to shimmer as if it forced its way through a translucent veil.

This, Tempera thought, was the perfect moment when the streets, strangely luminous in the dusk, were coloured pink as if they had soaked up the sun and would store it until morning.

The fading light glowed from walls of saffron, rose-red, and peach, and the pavements shone almost as though the lava remembered prehistoric fires.

St. Peter's Dome was now purple across the Tiber and first one church-bell and then another cast a silver note into the air.

The bells of Rome were ringing the *Angelus*—the Ave Maria—and another day of Italian life had passed.

But for Tempera life was beginning.

She heard a step behind her and although her whole body became tense she did not turn but waited shyly for him as she felt she had waited from the moment she was born.

He came to her side, and she heard his deep voice ask:

"Are you real? Or are you the angel I have always

been seeking and who now I have found in the country to which she belongs?"

Tempera smiled and turned her face.

Then because he was better-looking, larger, and more overpowering even than she remembered, she found it hard to move.

She looked up into his eyes and thought they held a touch of fire from the last glow of the sinking sun.

"I love you!" the Duke said. "I could not believe that days could pass so slowly until I saw you again."

He put out his arms as he spoke and drew her close to him, then his lips were on hers.

He was part of the golden glow over the city, part of the dusk, the statues, and the cypress trees; they were encompassed by the spiritual wonder they had felt when they looked at the picture they both loved.

"I love you! I love you!"

Tempera was not certain if she said the words or they were spoken in her heart, but she knew the Duke could hear them.

He raised his head and with his arms enfolding her drew her closer to the stone balustrade so that they could look down together at the silver ribbon of the Tiber moving slowly past the Churches, Castles, Domes, and Towers.

"Tomorrow morning," he said, "we will attend your Stepmother's wedding, and afterwards, my darling heart, I have arranged ours."

"Tomorrow?" Tempera asked.

"I cannot wait any longer," the Duke answered, "and we are going to spend our honeymoon, you and I, looking at some of the famous pictures of Italy which will speak to us as your father said they would."

"I can imagine nothing more . . . wonderful than to . . . look with you and listen to what they have to say," Tempera replied.

"We will finish our tour of the Masterpieces of Italy in Florence," the Duke continued. "And when finally we start the journey home we will stop in Paris to see your portrait in the Louvre."

Tempera gave a little cry of happiness, then she said:

"Papa showed it to me when I was ten years old, and told me that one day I would resemble the angel, but I thought no-one else would ever see the likeness."

The Duke drew her closer to him and his lips were on the softness of her cheek before he said:

"I was nine, or perhaps a year younger, when my father took me and half a dozen other boys, mostly cousins, to the Louvre. There was a painter he was trying to help, Antonio was his name, and he told us that if we each chose a picture we liked he would paint a reproduction of it for us to hang in our bed-rooms."

Tempera held her breath. She knew what was coming.

"My playmates had a variety of different tastes," the Duke went on, "most of them liking battles, some preferring allegorical pictures. But I remember one of my cousins rather surprised my father because he asked for Boucher's *Birth of Diana*."

He kissed Tempera's cheek again as he said:

"You know already what I chose."

"The picture that is on the wall in your Château."

"When we reached Leonardo da Vinci's painting," the Duke said, "I pointed to it and told my father: 'That is what I want!'

" 'It is a big picture!' Antonio grumbled. 'It will take me a long time.'

" 'I do not want the whole picture,' I replied. 'Just the angel.'

"My father was surprised.

" 'Just the angel, Velde, but why?'

" 'No-one could be more beautiful!' I answered, and my father said no more."

"I have always wished that I could be even half as beautiful," Tempera murmured.

"It will take me a lifetime to tell you, my darling," the Duke answered, "not only how beautiful you are, but how grateful I am to the fates that I have found you."

He drew in his breath before he said:

"I could hardly credit you were real when you turned towards me in the garden with that half-smile on your lips and the light in your eyes that da Vinci had painted five hundred years ago."

"I loved you as . . . soon as I saw . . . you," Tempera said in a low voice, "though I would not admit it to myself. But when we were together in the moonlight I felt as if there was no need for words between us, and although you did not . . . touch me, I felt as if I were in your . . . arms."

She blushed as she spoke and would have hidden her face against him, but the Duke put his fingers under her little pointed chin and lifted her face up to his.

"We have found each other," he said, "that is all that matters. I know everything you think, my darling, everything you feel, because they are my feelings and my thoughts too."

"Did you know that I was in . . . danger?" Tempera asked.

She relived for a second that terrifying moment when she had looked down at the precipice beneath her and knew she would die on the rocks.

"I had gone to bed but I could not sleep," the Duke answered. "That was nothing new: I had lain awake thinking of you ever since I found you in the garden. But that night it was almost as if you were calling to me, telling me you were worried."

"I thought you . . . hated me for what you . . . thought I had . . . done," Tempera said in a low voice.

She had not meant to speak of that agonising moment when the Duke had seen her on the stairs coming down from Lord Eustace's bed-room, but now she felt there must be no secrets between them.

"Forgive me, my Dearest Dream," the Duke pleaded. "It was only for one crazy instant that I was blinded by jealousy. Then when I came from Lady Holcombe's room I looked for you, knowing that to doubt your purity and innocence was to defame my love."

Tempera heard the pain in his voice and knew that it hurt him to speak of what he must have thought of as a betrayal of everything they both held sacred.

"You had gone," the Duke said, "but I meant to find you the next day, however cleverly you hid yourself."

"I was ... determined that you would not ... find me."

"I would have found you. Nothing would have kept me from you," he said firmly.

She thought he would kiss her but although his lips brushed hers he went on as if his story must have an ending.

"When the Count came to my room to tell me that Eustace had gone downstairs, I knew then that you had discovered, just as we had, that some of the pictures were fakes and that that alone was the explanation of your being in the Tower."

"I thought it was safe to search while the servants were having dinner," Tempera explained. "But I was looking only for the *Madonna in the Church*."

"It was very perceptive of you to realise that that was a fake," the Duke exclaimed. "Vincenzo says that one is the best copy of the three and he is certain that it would deceive most experts."

"It did not deceive me," Tempera said, "because the feeling I had and which ... you had too ... was not there."

"It was amazingly clever of you, my precious," the Duke said. "The Count noticed first the Raphel, then the Cristus."

"And you were sure it was Lord Eustace?"

"There was no-one else in need of money—except yourself."

"And you did not suspect me?"

"Not for a moment," he said. "No-one could look like my angel, my very own angel, and be anything but perfect."

Tempera blushed and he went on:

"The Count and I decided that we must catch Eustace red-handed. It would have been useless just to confront him with the theft. He would only have denied it and we had no proof. But we assumed that even if he had already disposed of his first haul, he would be greedy enough to take others."

"He had brought only three fakes with him," Tempera said.

"We know that now," the Duke answered, "but we were waiting, thinking he would go downstairs, and when he did so the Count, as arranged, came to my room and we followed him."

"To . . . save me," Tempera whispered.

"Even now I can hardly bear to think that if we had been a few seconds later I would have lost you," the Duke said.

He made a sound that was half a groan, then he was kissing her wildly, passionately, frantically, as if even now he was not certain she was safe.

His lips were fierce and demanding but she was not afraid.

This was love as she had always known it would be, not only spiritual, but also fierce and tempestuous, burning with the heat of the sun as well as the silver serenity of the moon.

The fire within the Duke lit an answering flame within herself and she felt as if her whole body came alive to glow with a radiance and luminosity that was part of the Divine.

The Duke kissed her until she felt as if he carried her up towards the stars overhead and they were part of them.

Then when he raised his lips from hers he said:

"Tomorrow night you will be mine and I can prove my love, my precious one. It is so complete, so overwhelming, that only when we are man and wife will I be able to express the depth, height, and breadth of it."

"I want to ... belong to you. I want to be with ... you."

Her voice was almost as passionate as his.

"You are so lovely, my darling heart," the Duke said, "but we both know there is something between us that is more important than beauty, something indefinable, and yet very real."

She saw him smile as he added:

"Your father told you to look and listen, which we will always do together; but he forgot to add one other word—a word which is the most important of all."

"What is that?" Tempera asked.

"We will look, listen—and love!" the Duke answered. "All I ask of the future, my precious angel, is that we shall do those three things together."

"It is what I want ... too," Tempera wished to say, but his lips were on hers and it was impossible to speak.

She could only look at him with her eyes—listen to him with her heart, and love him completely with her soul and her body.

She was his and he was hers for all eternity.

ABOUT THE AUTHOR

BARBARA CARTLAND, the celebrated romantic author, historian, playwright, lecturer, political speaker and television personality, has now written over 150 books. Miss Cartland has had a number of historical books published and several biographical ones, including that of her brother, Major Ronald Cartland, who was the first Member of Parliament to be killed in the War. This book had a Foreword by Sir Winston Churchill.

In private life, Barbara Cartland, who is a Dame of the Order of St. John of Jerusalem, has fought for better conditions and salaries for Midwives and Nurses. As President of the Royal College of Midwives (Hertfordshire Branch), she has been invested with the first Badge of Office ever given in Great Britain, which was subscribed to by the Midwives themselves. She has also championed the cause for old people and founded the first Romany Gypsy Camp in the world.

Barbara Cartland is deeply interested in Vitamin Therapy and is President of the British National Association for Health.